Book of Legends:
Volume 0

First Edition March 2023

ISBN: 978-1-915727-01-5

Cover Art: Ralph Horsley
Interior Art: Ralph Horsley, Michael Rechlin
World Map: Tiffany Munro
Character Art: Michael Rechlin

DungeonCraft Publishing

ORBIS TERRARUM IMPERII

ONE KINGDOM RÌYÈ

TERRA NOVUM

Portus Nova

AGER MERIDIANUS

Pratumium

WESTERN ETERNAL EMPIRE

Yax Mutal

MAGNA ARBORES

Flumenium

N

THRONE OF THE JAGUAR

BOOK OF LEGENDS CHARACTER SHEET

NAME:_____

RACE:_____

PATRON GOD:_____ KEYWORD:_____

ARMOUR RATING

ABILITIES

	LEVEL	MODIFIER	TOTAL
LORE			
MYSTICAL			
WEAPONS			
AGILITY			
DEXTERITY			
KNOWLEDGE			
NATURE			
PERCEPTION			
PHYSICAL			
SCAVENGING			
SOCIAL			

MAX HEALTH

ABILITY LEVELS	PURCHASED	MODIFIER	TOTAL

HEALTH

ABILITY POINTS

PRAYERS

SKILLS

- ACUTE HEARING
- AETHERWEAVER
- ALCHEMY
- ARTEFACT
- ATHLETICS
- BARTER
- BRAWLING
- CLIMBING
- CONSTITUTION
- CONTORTION
- DECEPTION
- DETECT
- DISARM TRAPS
- DUAL WEAPONS

- ETIQUETTE
- EXPERT PALATE
- FORAGING
- FORGERY
- GADGETRY
- HERBALISM
- HISTORY
- HUNTING
- INFERNALS
- INTIMIDATION
- JINSHU YU ROU
- LOCKPICK
- MAGIC SENSE
- MAGICAL ITEMS

- MELEE WEAPONS
- MINING
- MYTH
- NAVIGATION
- NIGHT VISION
- PERSUASION
- RANGED WEAPONS
- REFLEXES
- RELIGION
- REPAIR
- RUNELORE
- SCIENCE
- SIXTH SENSE
- SLEIGHT OF HAND

- SMITHING
- SNEAK
- STREETWISE
- STRENGTH
- SURVIVAL
- SWIMMING
- TACTICS
- THE TRUTH
- TRACKING
- TREASURE SEEKING
- TRINKET GATHERING
- WORLD
- ZOOLOGY

INVENTORY

ITEMS EQUIPPED

ARMOUR..

SHIELD..

WEAPON..

DUAL WEAPON...

HEAD..

NECK...

ARMS..

BODY..

LEGS...

FEET..

RING...

RING...

BACKPACK EQUIPMENT

OTHER ITEMS

CONSUMABLES

PROVISIONS (MAX 14)

RESOURCES

CRYSTALS (MAX 50)

SILVER DENARII

TREASURY

INCOME & EXPENSES

UNIQUE MASTERIES

CONDITIONS

POWERS

TIME TRACK

VOL 0 CHAPTER

I ☐ ☐ ☐ ☐ ☐ ☐ ☐ ☐ ☐ ☐ ☐ 36   REST ☐

II ☐ ☐ ☐ ☐ ☐ ☐ ☐ ☐ ☐ ☐ 72   REST ☐

III ☐ ☐ ☐ ☐ ☐ A ☐ ☐ ☐ ☐ 101   REST ☐

VOLUME 0 CODEWORDS

☐ APRON ☐ BENCH ☐ CABAL ☐ DEITY ☐ EXALT ☐ FEAST ☐ GRADE ☐ HALVE

☐ INGOT ☐ JEWEL ☐ KNAVE ☐ LUCID ☐ MINOR ☐ NOVEL ☐ OUTER ☐ PINCH

☐ QUILL ☐ REMIT ☐ SMART ☐ TREAD ☐ URBAN ☐ VAGUE ☐ WAVER ☐ YOUTH

JOURNAL

COMPANION

ARMOUR RATING

NAME:_____ TOTAL [ ]

ABILITIES

TOTAL [ ]

MAX HEALTH [ ]

HEALTH [ ]

SKILLS

INVENTORY

NOTES

_____ [ ]
_____ [ ]
_____ [ ]
_____ [ ]
_____ [ ]
_____ [ ]
_____ [ ]

ON COMPANION'S DEATH, TURN TO SECTION_____ IN VOLUME_____

A	B	C	D

E	F	G	H
			POWER / REPUTATION

I	J	K	L
		POWER / REPUTATION	

M	N	O CORDI	P

Q	R	S	T
POWER / REPUTATION	POWER / REPUTATION		I / II

U	V	W	X
			POWER / REPUTATION

Name:	Aelina Rutilius
Race:	Peregrine Alta
God:	Ceres [Earth]

Abilities

Lore	0
Mystical	0
Weapons	2
Agility	2
Dexterity	0
Knowledge	1
Nature	1
Perception	0
Physical	2
Scavenging	0
Social	2
Max Health	26
Skills:	Athletics, Etiquette, Herbalism, Intimidation, Melee Weapons, Persuasion, Reflexes, Smithing, Swimming, Tactics.
Ability Points	2

Notes

Aelina's early years in the empire's east were a comfortable start in life, yet it was a dull and uninspiring existence for someone with such ambitions. Her father, a high-ranking tribunus in the XLV Legion, brought his entire family to his posting in Athenae, and they enjoyed the more relaxing aspects of army life in this peaceful province.

Splitting her time between weapons training and battle tactics during the day, and the endless social gatherings that marked life in the upper tiers of society, she gained a well-rounded experience as a young adult. An experience that her father hoped would lead her to high offices within the legion, and maybe even the senate.

Sadly for him, Aelina's thirst for experience and adventure led her to fill a small backpack one day with the bare minimum of possessions. She did not want an easy life gifted to her, and a small amount of coin gained her passage on a vessel heading west towards Italia.

Name:	Edwin Corbridge
Race:	Human
God:	None

Abilities

Lore	0
Mystical	2
Weapons	1
Agility	0
Dexterity	2
Knowledge	1
Nature	1
Perception	1
Physical	0
Scavenging	0
Social	1
Max Health	24
Skills:	Alchemy, Barter, Expert Palate, Disarm Traps, Melee Weapons, Repair, Runelore, Science, Zoology.
Ability Points	4

Notes

Edwin was the eldest child born into a family of farmers near the city of Camulodunon, situated in the south-east of the province of Britannia. His interests and learning at an early age naturally reflected that upbringing, and his future as head of the family farm was all but assured.

His discovery of several bright red crystals buried deep in a field one spring caused his future to travel a different path. The tangible power of the crystals mesmerised Edwin, and he spent time away from the markets of Londinium to procure texts that would allow him to unleash their potential.

The Collegia Naturae in the provincial capital would not contemplate admitting someone with such a background into their distinguished ranks. It, therefore, took several years of self-study, and more than one blackened and charred barn, before he gained the confidence to travel to the heart of the empire and learn more.

Name:	Epia Lanatus
Race:	Terra Volas
God:	Mercury [Air]

Abilities

Lore	1
Mystical	1
Weapons	1
Agility	1
Dexterity	0
Knowledge	0
Nature	1
Perception	2
Physical	1
Scavenging	2
Social	0
Max Health	25
Skills:	Acute Hearing, Constitution, Contortion, Hunting, Magical Items, Melee Weapons, Myth, Navigation, Sixth Sense, Trinket Gathering
Ability Points	0
Powers	Feather

Notes

The Cacumen district of Lugdunum, perched hundreds of feet above the stone buildings of the old city below, was Epia's remote home for almost all her life, yet a nagging desire to explore was always present.

Her six-year compulsory service in the city militia was varied and interesting, and this kept her yearnings at bay for that while. Epia showed good aptitude in almost all disciplines, which sent her career on a path that saw her undertake many roles within the militia, such as warrior, ranger, priest, and magi, all within the half-decade of her service.

When this term ended, Epia's need for experience and mental stimulation caused her to look further into the world. Heading to the heart of the empire was an obvious choice for her next steps.

Name:	Brenent Geirr Arcus
Race:	Durum
God:	Neptune [Water]

Abilities

Lore	0
Mystical	0
Weapons	3
Agility	0
Dexterity	0
Knowledge	0
Nature	1
Perception	0
Physical	2
Scavenging	0
Social	1
Max Health	26
Skills:	Brawling, Dual Weapons, Melee Weapons, Ranged Weapons, Strength, Streetwise, Survival.
Ability Points	1

Notes

Brenent was born into a large family of stonemasons and labourers in the mountaintop durum stronghold of Culmen Fortis. His imposing frame, even compared with his durum brethren, invited much trouble and he was a well know face among the magistrates.

It was this environment that caused him to depart from the city, bidding a sad farewell to the family that fully expected him to continue in their business. Brenent knew he either must leave or end up a resident in the city gaols.

He travelled the lands from Olbia to the far east to the southern African provinces, plying his trade, and conflict was never far from his side. Guard, gladiator, legionary, and bounty hunter were some of his many vocations, and his life remained transient. He never spent more than several months to a year working in any one area.

Stepping on a ship in Carthago marked the end of his most recent spell of work. The central province of Italia awaits.

Name:	Abar-Tetu Khentep
Race:	Human
God:	Khepri [Fire]

Abilities

Lore	1
Mystical	0
Weapons	2
Agility	0
Dexterity	2
Knowledge	2
Nature	0
Perception	1
Physical	0
Scavenging	2
Social	1
Max Health	28
Skills:	Deception, Foraging, Forgery, History, Melee Weapons, Night Vision, Ranged Weapons, Religion, Sleight of Hand, Treasure Seeking, World.
Ability Points	0

Notes

Abar-Tetu was born into slavery in the city of Memphis in the province of Ægyptus. From an early age, she was shown to be a bright and capable individual with extraordinary talents in both language and mathematics.

Destined to spend her life as a scribe in the servitude of one of the wealthy families of the city, she was freed in her seventeenth year when armies of the Greater Arscacid Dynasty crossed the Nile and sacked the city in their push to claim the lands west of the river.

Never abandoning her faith in the sun god Khepri, she narrowly escaped the battle and the carnage wrought upon the city after. Pretending to be a Persian slave returning to Pasargadae, Abar-Tetu spent the next years practising her martial skills while heading out of the provinces and into the heart of the empire.

Name:	Marcus Cornelius Philo
Race:	Peregrine Agilis
God:	Jupiter [Aether]

Abilities

Lore	2
Mystical	0
Weapons	1
Agility	1
Dexterity	1
Knowledge	1
Nature	0
Perception	2
Physical	0
Scavenging	1
Social	0
Max Health	24
Skills:	Artefact, Climbing, Detect, Gadgetry, Infernals, Lockpick, Melee Weapons, Sixth Sense, Treasure Seeking.
Ability Points:	5

Notes

A devout and observant worshipper of Jupiter, the king of gods, Marcus knew from an early age that he was born to spread his beliefs throughout the world to save a crumbling society and the people within.

Proudly receiving his focus in the temple of Jupiter in Roma, he headed at once, bright and enthusiastic, into the empire. However, it took a short time for cynicism to embed itself, and Marcus eventually grew weary of the futility of his mission.

Realising that hard lives breed hard people, and many of them, while not dishonest, needed to survive. They would happily take what is yours to make their lives a little easier. Faced with this contradiction, Marcus is now as likely to offer you a blessing for alms as he is to take your money anyway.

The empire, compared with the province of Italia and in particular the capital of Roma, offered little in the way of rewards, and Marcus eventually planned his return journey.

Introduction

Welcome to Book of Legends: The Eternal Empire, a series of exciting open-world gamebooks where you are the story's hero. This volume is a short prologue to the main story, designed to introduce you to the game's design and offering a flavour of a wider world, packed with hours of adventure and intrigue.

You play the role of a brave adventurer, travelling a world much like our own many hundreds of years ago. The Roman Empire has flourished and expanded into the Americas, and magic has both blessed and cursed the planet in unequal measures.

You will determine not only the fates of your character and those around them, but you will even direct the course of entire empires.

Will you be a champion of virtue, fighting selflessly for good causes, or are you only interested in fame, riches, and power? The choice is yours.

Before you embark on your adventures, you will need some six-sided dice. If you own a physical copy of this book, grab a pencil and eraser, too.

Your Character

The character is your alter-ago in these adventures and the lead actor in this story. Someone who left their homeland in search of adventure and will succeed or die from the decisions you take.

To begin your adventures as swiftly as possible, take any of the six pre-generated characters before this page and copy the details into page 1 of your character sheets.

Visit **www.bookoflegends.co.uk** to print these character sheets or download to use on an electronic device. It will be easier to use separate character sheets, either physical or electronic copies, as you will refer to them frequently during your adventures, saving you from having to move back and forth in the same book.

The following are the steps to build your customised character.

1. Choose your race.

2. Gain free levels for that race's innate strengths.

3. All characters gain level 1 in Weapons.

4. Gain 1 further level in any of the three primary abilities.

5. Spend 36 ability points to increase levels in all abilities.

6. Calculate Max Health.

7. Pick skills for each ability.

8. Choose your patron god (optional).

Abilities

Every character has ability scores that represent the quality of their physical, mental, and spiritual attributes.

The first three primary abilities are tested constantly during your adventures.

LORE - Your knowledge of religion in general and the strength of your own faith in particular. Used to call upon the favours of the gods.

MYSTICAL - Your understanding of the power of arcane crystals and their effects in the world. Used to cast spells.

WEAPONS - Your competence at fighting with weapons. Often used when encountering the many vile creatures and dangerous people inhabiting these lands who would wish you harm. You begin your adventures automatically at level 1 in the Weapons ability.

Several secondary abilities will be frequently called upon, but not necessarily in combative circumstances.

AGILITY - Your body's grace and nimbleness. Offers a defensive bonus at level 3 (see the Combat section).

DEXTERITY - Your deftness with your hands.

KNOWLEDGE - The amount of information you have built up on various subjects over your life.

NATURE - Your experience in the wilderness and your understanding of animals.

PERCEPTION - The keenness of your eye.

PHYSICAL - Your fortitude, strength, and endurance.

SCAVENGING - Your talent in finding useful resources in your environment.

SOCIAL - Your charisma and skills in communication.

In normal circumstances for any character, each ability has 5 levels of competence with a practised novice starting at level 1, rising to level 5 for a master of the craft.

Anyone at level 0 in an ability is a beginner. They are not wholly ineffective, but will be disadvantaged in any tests that require that ability.

The minimum modified level for all abilities is 0. The maximum modified level for all abilities is double the base level.

Two further values represent your capacity for surviving damage.

MAX HEALTH - The total amount of damage a healthy and rested individual can take before they are dead.

HEALTH - The amount of damage you can presently suffer before death occurs. This might be lower than Max Health because of illness or injury, or sometimes higher owing to magical effects.

When you are instructed to gain or lose Health in the story, add or remove that number from this score. If your Health goes to zero, you are dead and the adventure ends.

Human Evolution

Over a millennium ago, a cataclysmic event called the Divine Fire created mutations that branched humanity into several evolutionary races and species. The speed of this evolution was quicker than anyone had witnessed in nature, and over just a few generations, several distinct racial groups emerged and prospered.

The following describes the dominant races that populate the planet today. Pick one and enter this at the top of page 1 of your character sheets. For each innate strength, gain the free levels noted in the respective abilities.

HUMAN (pl. Humans)

Humans are the progenitor race from which all others evolved following the Fire. Numerous and adaptable, they happily exist in most environments and thrive in any land they call home.

Innate strengths. Dexterity (level 2), Social (level 1).

PEREGRINE ALTA (pl. Peregrine altas)

Intelligent and graceful, altas are tall blueish and purple-skinned humanoids found in many upper echelons of power. Their black eyes and feline teeth are unsettling to many, but they are patient and civilised unless provoked. Emperor Romulus Himself is a rare example of an apex peregrine alta.

Innate strengths. Knowledge (level 1), Social (level 2).

PEREGRINE AGILIS (pl. Peregrine agilia)

The agilia are the thin and short contrast to their ruling class cousins with the same blue skin and deep black eyes. Their quick minds are matched only by their sprightly bodies and keen vision. While they lack the stature of their loftier brethren, their adaptable and somewhat chaotic outlook means they thrive as well as their human counterparts in all environments.

Innate strengths. Agility (level 1), Perception (level 2).

DURUM (pl. Durum)

Hardy and strong, durum are grey-skinned, of similar height to humans, but much broader with a thicker bone and muscle structure. Their outlook on life matches the environments in which they thrive, remote and bleak. They centre their societies around tribal boundaries and are fiercely loyal to family and clan.

Innate strengths. Nature (level 1), Physical (level 2).

TERRA VOLAS (pl. Terra volatis)

The terra volatis are a winged race of avian humanoids who, because of their dense bone structure compared with birds, cannot fly nearly as well. They can hover in the air for several seconds and use their wings to lessen the impacts of falls. They share many of the same behaviours as predator avian species and live remotely in small family units in the wilderness.

Innate strengths. Perception (level 2), Scavenging (level 1).

Add **Feather** to the Powers section of your character sheets if you choose this race.

Ability Points

You have 35 ability points to spend on improving your abilities.

All abilities will be used frequently throughout your adventures, and you will not be disadvantaged choosing to practice one ability over another.

> Optional rule: To increase the difficulty of your game, take only 28 ability points. Mark the 7 points you did not use against the 🐃 symbol (I) on your character sheet. In future, for every multiple of 5 ability points awarded on a single occasion, take only 4 and add 1 point to that symbol.

Parents teach children martial skills at an early age in this dangerous and unforgiving world. All characters begin the story at level 1 in the Weapons ability.

Next, take one free level, worth 15 points, in any primary ability: Lore, Mystical or Weapons. This additional level represents further training your character has undertaken before the events of these volumes begin.

Then, spend your ability points improving your ability levels. The costs to raise the levels of abilities are below along with the Max Health increase with every level gained.

Abilities	Level Cost					Max Health
	1	2	3	4	5	
Lore	15	20	30	50	70	+2
Mystical	15	20	30	50	80	+2
Weapons	Free	15	30	50	70	+4
Agility	6	10	16	24	36	+1
Dexterity	4	7	11	17	25	+1
Knowledge	3	5	8	12	18	+1
Nature	4	6	10	14	22	+1
Perception	4	7	11	17	25	+1
Physical	5	8	13	19	29	+1
Scavenging	3	5	8	12	18	+1
Social	4	6	10	14	22	+1

Example: To increase Knowledge to level 1 costs 3 ability points. From level 1 to level 3 is 13 points (5 points to level 2, plus 8 points to level 3).

Max Health has a base value of 10 points. Increase this by the value in the last column above for each level you have attained in that ability, including any free levels gained at the start of the character creation process. *For example, level 4 in Weapons increases Max Health by 16 points.*

Write this total value against Max Health on the character sheet. It should be within a range of 19 to 29 if you spend most or all of your ability points.

Max Health does not increase if you gain a modifier to an ability, only for actual levels attained. It will increase if you are awarded and then spend ability points in the future.

You may spend 5 ability points to increase your Max Health by 1 point. Write the total of points you have gained in the Max Health modifier box named 'Purchased'.

Your Health is at its maximum value when you start the game. It cannot go above its maximum value unless specifically stated in the story.

You cannot use spells or prayers unless you have at least level 1 in the Mystical or Lore abilities, respectively.

Record any unused points under the Ability Points section on your character sheet.

You will gain ability points during the upcoming adventures as you complete key moments in your quests. You can spend ability points on secondary abilities if you take a *full rest* (see the section on Resting later), or if the text says you can spend ability points at that time.

The three primary abilities of Lore, Mystical, and Weapons require specialist training and funding to increase levels, and the text will inform you when you can train in these, usually in or near population centres.

Skills

As you gain experience by adventuring in the world, you also gain skills. These allow for interesting opportunities throughout the story that would otherwise be more difficult to obtain or simply unavailable to you. A tavern keeper might impart extra information when questioned, or you could recognise a weakness in a particular species of animal you must fight. They also provide occasional bonus modifiers when your abilities are tested.

For every level that you have in an ability, you may choose one skill from that ability from the list below. There are five skills for each ability, thus you will have all skills when you reach level 5.

Mark the checkboxes against your choices in the Skills section of your character sheet.

Lore

Artefact	Your expertise with religious artefacts and relics, including details of their powers, history, and creation.
Infernals	Your understanding of infernals, powerful creatures who inhabit the underworld and their commanders, the infernal gods themselves.
Myth	Your knowledge of esoteric creatures, legendary individuals, and fabled stories, whose very existence is the subject of fierce debate.
Religion	Your general knowledge of the myriad religions in the world. This represents a scholarly understanding of these religions rather than a belief.
The Truth	Only available when you achieve an unmodified level 5 in the Lore ability. When you select this skill at level 5, the text will inform you of its effects.

Mystical

Aether-weaver	Only available when you achieve an unmodified level 5 in the Mystical ability. When you select this skill at level 5, the text will inform you of its effects.
Alchemy	Your talent brewing potions given the correct ingredients and equipment.
Magic Sense	The innate feeling you have of the power emanated from magical sources such as crystals, runes, and creatures or items with a magical origin.
Magical Items	Your expertise in creating magical weapons, apparel, and other objects.
Runelore	You can inscribe scrolls and items with powerful runes that store magical effects.

Weapons

Dual Weapons	Only available when you achieve an unmodified level 3 in the Weapons ability. You are proficient in using two weapons with a keyword of [Small], either melee and/or ranged, simultaneously in combat.
Jinshu Yu Rou	A mysterious martial art developed in the One Kingdom, only available when you achieve an unmodified level 5 in the Weapons ability. When you select this skill at level 5, the text will inform you of its effects.
Melee Weapons	You can wield hand-to-hand weapons proficiently. To use a melee weapon without this skill requires a 5+ rather than a 4+ in combat to hit successfully.
Ranged Weapons	You can employ ranged weapons proficiently. Using a ranged weapon without this skill requires a 5+ rather than a 4+ in combat to hit successfully.
Tactics	You fight more effectively with others. If you are in combat with at least one companion or ally, add +1 modifier to your Weapons ability.

Agility

Athletics	You are of superior fitness, able to run fast, and maintain this speed over long distances.
Climbing	Your ability to climb vertical surfaces given the right environment and equipment.
Contortion	You have a flexible and supple body, to help negotiate narrow and awkward gaps.
Reflexes	The speed at which you can react to your environment.
Sneak	Your proficiency in moving silently, without being spotted.

Dexterity

Disarm traps	Your talent in making traps safe.
Forgery	Your skill in creating and spotting fake versions of official documents, seals, and other objects.
Lockpick	Your ability to bypass non-magical locks.
Repair	You can repair a wide variety of simple items. This does not include weapons or armour (see the Smithing skill).
Sleight of Hand	Your gift in performing hidden actions with your hands, and spotting others attempting the same.

Knowledge

Gadgetry   With access to a workshop, and given the correct schematics and components, you are proficient in creating and maintaining complex machinery.

History   Your knowledge of the past times of the world.

Science   The aptitude you show in the physics, chemistry, and biology disciplines.

Smithing   You are adept at creating and repairing weapons, armour, and similar metal and non-metal items.

World   Your awareness of today's world, its locales, and important individuals.

Nature

Herbalism   Your understanding of the properties of herbs, and the combinations of such, in providing useful effects for both remedies and poisons.

Navigation   Your wayfinding ability and skill in travelling across the world rapidly and safely.

Survival   Your ability to live off the land or sea. A **Short Rest** (see later) brings the character up to 14 Health rather than 10. Additionally, health loss from a lack of provisions is lessened.

Tracking   Your skill in following people and animals through most environments.

Zoology   Your knowledge of creatures, animals, and sentient races and species.

Perception

Acute Hearing   Your ability to discern faint sounds and to separate them from background noise (e.g. Overhearing a hushed conversation in a loud, crowded room).

Detect   The keenness of your eye in spotting things of interest in your immediate surroundings, for example detecting traps and secret doors.

Expert Palate   With a refined sense of taste and smell, you can identify many flavours and aromas, and distinguish individual components in complex blends.

Night Vision   You can see more clearly in darkness.

Sixth Sense   Your unconscious ability to sense something of importance with no obvious external stimuli.

Physical

Brawling   Your brute strength is a weapon. You are not penalised for fighting without a weapon and you require a roll of 4+ to hit an enemy in combat.

Constitution   Your capacity to survive diseases, venoms, and poisons.

Intimidation   How threatening you can appear and how well you can use this to persuade others through fear.

Strength   You are physically strong, carrying heavy objects with ease and breaking down sturdy doors with no effort.

Swimming   Everybody can float and move in water, but with this skill, you swim in difficult circumstances, hold your breath for longer, and traverse substantial bodies of water.

Scavenging

Foraging	Your talent in finding useful herbs, berries, and crops from your environment searches.
Hunting	Your ability to obtain meat and hides from your environment searches.
Mining	Your skill in locating useful ore from your environment searches.
Treasure Seeking	Your aptitude in finding valuable objects and precious items from your environment searches.
Trinket Gathering	Your expertise acquiring useful magical objects from your environment searches.

Social

Barter	Your ability to negotiate.
Deception	Your gift lying convincingly and detecting when others are being untruthful.
Etiquette	Your talent blending in with upper-class society and the knowledge of those traditions.
Persuasion	Your capability in convincing others to do your bidding.
Streetwise	Your experience of life in a working-class, urban environment.

Religion

Faith in higher powers has been a key foundation for civilisations throughout history and this has only strengthened since the cataclysmic events a thousand years ago. As a citizen or subject of one of the four great powers, you have an extensive choice of deities from the pantheons of the empires below for your patron god.

If you do not have any levels in the Lore ability, this adds flavour to your character rather than influencing the game to any degree.

Any character with at least level 1 in Lore can call upon the powers of their patron god. These otherworldly effects are gifted from ancient relics called a focus, angular and mysteriously shaped pieces of metal that grafts to the skin of the faithful and cannot be removed without destroying the artefact and killing the host.

Examples of deities of the Great Empires are below. Add the name of your chosen god to your character sheet. If you have at least level 1 in Lore, also add the keyword of this god to your character sheet. You may not change or add a god or keyword after character creation unless the text states otherwise.

This list is not exhaustive and merely gives a flavour of the thousands of historical gods. Feel free to use a different god than those listed below, or to change the keyword if they have more than one facet.

The keyword of your character's god is the most important information used in the game. The god's name will not give you benefits or penalties.

For example. A priest of Huracan, the Mayan god of fire, would gain benefits from worshipping at a temple of Vulcan, the Roman god of the same element.

Huracan also represents the wind or storms (the origin of the word 'Hurricane'), and the priest would not gain benefits from a temple of Huracan dedicated to that god's 'Air' aspect.

Keyword	Eternal Empire	Greater Arsacid Dynasty	Throne of the Jaguar	One Kingdom Riye
Aether	Jupiter	Ahura Mazda	Itzamná	Shangdi
Air	Mercury	Vayu	Kukulcán	Dianmu
Earth	Ceres	Tishtrya	Hun Nal Ye	Sheji
Fire	Vulcan	Atar	Huracan	Zhurong
Infernals*	Orcus	Angra Mainyu	Ah Puch	Yan Wang
Water	Neptune	Apam Napat	Chaac	Longwang

* The worship of infernal gods is specifically outlawed across the empire, but you are free to choose a god with a keyword of [Infernal] if your character has that outlook. While this worship is not necessarily a trait of an evildoer, you are encouraged not to advertise this in public.

Rules of Play

General Rules

To play the game, you read from the beginning of a body of text called a section, numbered in this volume from 1 to 200, until you reach an instruction or decision point.

You must complete instructions in the order in which you reach them in that section's text. You may pass over decision points when you first read them, coming back after looking at the rest of the options and then deciding on your course of action.

These instructions or decisions will usually require you to either update your character sheet or turning to a new section number. The following pages explain the more complex situations you will encounter.

A summary of the rules can be found on this volume's inside back cover for quick reference.

Ability Checks

At many points in the story, you must perform actions where the outcome is uncertain and depend on your abilities and skills, along with an amount of luck.

If the text instructs you to make a check against an ability, roll a number of dice equal to your level in that ability, plus or minus any modifiers.

You will always have a minimum of 1 die for an ability check, even at a modified level of zero or below.

Any score of 4+ grants one success, and the text will note how many successes you require to pass the check.

If you have a modified level of 0 in an ability, roll 1 die and record a single success on a score of 5+ only.

You can choose to gain bonuses to these checks by applying powers from crystals using your Mystical ability or from Prayers using your Lore ability. You may not use both crystals and Prayers in a single ability check. The section on magic has more details.

Positive bonuses do not stack and you will normally use the highest value modifier available. For example, you only gain a bonus of +3 to Weapons when drinking a Potion of Might (+3 Weapons) and a using a fine Sword (+2 Weapons). Status buffs, negative modifiers, and modifiers in the text will further modify the value for the ability check.

Combat

The Combat Round

The Empire's lands are unimaginably dangerous, even to seasoned travellers, and the number of people and creatures who wish you harm are legion. You will often face these situations, and when the text instructs you to fight one or more enemies, the encounter occurs in combat rounds.

You, the player, acts first and will complete all actions for your character, companion, and other allies in the combat before the enemy reacts.

The enemies, in the order they are listed in the text, complete their actions next.

The combat round then ends. A new round begins unless all enemies are dead, in which case you are victorious in the fight.

Each friendly combatant may perform one of the following actions during their turn. You choose who acts in which order, and if someone can act more than once in the round (for example using the Speed spell), then this second action also takes place when you choose.

- Perform a ranged or melee attack.

- Swap weapon. You may change one equipped weapon or shield for one other in your inventory.

- Use an item. Certain items can assist you in combat. The item's description will clearly state if an effect is usable in a combat round.

- Use one consumable or power.

- Cast a combat spell. See the section on magic.

- Use a unique mastery. Similar to powers and spells, a unique mastery is a rare capability the character possesses, and the description will state if you can use it in combat.

- Escape. If a fight is not progressing well, your character may escape as an action. The text will inform you if that option is available, and any events that happen if so.

Order of Battle

If there is one enemy, they will concentrate their attacks solely on the character and ignore companions or allies, as they are typically the most threatening opponent in the battle.

Multiple opponents are allocated equally among the friendly combatants at the start of the first round.

For each enemy, allocate the first listed to the character, the second to the companion, the third to ally #1 and so on. If there are any enemies remaining, allocate to the character, companion, ally in that order again until no more enemies remain or you reach the limit described below.

Do not change this order of battle for future rounds unless a fighter has no target and there is space available to attack an opponent. Any defeated combatants will be replaced if unused reinforcements are available, and in the order detailed above.

Typically, a maximum of 4 combatants can engage a single opponent with melee attacks in a single combat round. The text will explain any exceptions. Ranged attacks can be made at will by anyone against any opponent.

Some companions or allies are threatening enough they have special rules which cause them to become the primary target, such as the Astral Warrior spell. Here, the attacking order changes and this more threatening ally is attacked first.

If more than one companion or ally has this capability, prioritise the one with the higher Max Health value. If these are still equal, you may choose the order.

Attacks

An attack is considered an ability check for certain rules that may modify an ability of your choice when making a check (The **Well Rested** power when taking a full rest, for example).

To perform a melee attack in your turn, choose one enemy facing you in the order of battle.

Ranged combat attacks can be used against any enemy unless there are any restrictions explained in the text.

Roll a number of dice equal to the attacker's Weapons Ability adjusted for the Melee or Ranged modifier from their weapon, for example, **Dagger [Small Melee +0]** or **Greatsword [Large Melee +2]**. Roll 1 die if the attacker has a modified level of 0 in Weapons.

Any scores of 4+ are successful.

If the attacker has a Weapons ability of 0, score a success on a roll of 5+.

Using a melee or ranged weapon without the Melee Weapons or Ranged Weapons skill respectively requires a score of 5+ for success as well.

Likewise, if you have no weapon equipped and are fighting bare-handed (this is a melee attack), you also require a 5+ for success, even if you have the Melee Weapons skill. Ignore this penalty if you have the Brawling skill.

Your fists each have the keywords of [Small Melee +0] for any rules that require them, for example, the dual weapons rules.

For each success, remove a point of Health from the chosen enemy.

Once all actions are completed, your enemies then act. The text will inform you of any special abilities that your enemies can bring against you, but usually, your foes will just strike you with melee or ranged attacks.

Roll a number of dice equal to the first enemy's Weapons ability and count any 4+ as a success.

Then, roll a number of dice equal to your Armour Rating and reduce the number of the enemy's successes for every score of 4+ you roll. For the remaining dice that were successful, reduce your Health by that amount.

Continue down the list of enemies until all have completed their actions. If at least one enemy is still alive, a new combat round begins.

Rolls for your attacks and enemies' attacks, as well as your rolls for armour, all occur in one combat round. You can adjust all these with Prayers, but up to a maximum of 1 Prayer per level of your character's Lore ability in a single combat round.

Combat Example

Jorek is a warrior with a Weapons ability of 3 and wields a Light Mace [Small Melee +1]. He has the Melee Weapons skill and is fighting the following creature, a horrific hybrid of brown bear and tawny owl.

	Weapons	*Health*
Ursa Noctua	*4*	*10*

The player rolls 4 dice, 3 for the Weapons skill and 1 for the mace's modifier. They score a 6, 6, 4 and 3, which is 3 damage. They have reduced the Ursa Noctua to 7 Health.

The Ursa Noctua then attacks, rolling 4 dice with a 5, 4, 4 and 1. It also scores 3 successes. Jorek's Chain Shirt [Heavy Armour +2] allows the player to roll 2 dice for the armour rating, scoring a 6 and a 5. These two successes reduces the damage Jorek takes by 2.

The player reduces Jorek's Health by the 1 remaining success from the enemy's attack.

Defensive Agility Bonus

This bonus is only available at level 3 or higher in the Agility ability.

A character or companion who wears light or no armour have a lower likelihood of being hit by any retaliatory strikes from enemies. By keeping clear from hand-to-hand combat and staying out of sight of enemies with similar ranged capabilities, they are a harder target to hit.

If they use an item of armour equipped with the [Heavy Armour] keyword, they may not make use of the following benefits.

A character or companion who has not made a melee attack in this combat round may, once an enemy has successfully hit them with a damaging blow, roll a number of dice equal to half their Agility ability, rounded down.

On each roll of 6+, if wearing armour with keywords of [Light Armour], or a 5+ if not equipped with any items with a keyword of [Light Armour] or [Heavy Armour], they may reduce the number of successful hits by 1.

Items with a keyword of simply [Armour] are effectively weightless and gain protection with a roll of 5+.

Using damaging spells or other powers and items in an attack is not considered a melee attack for this extra protection, unless otherwise detailed.

These rolls are in addition to the protection they receive from their armour rating and are resolved before any protection from the armour itself. Therefore, a character would roll dice equal to half their Agility first to see if they can avoid any damaging blows. They would then roll for their armour rating to see if it had protected them against any remaining damage.

Dual Weapons

If you have the Dual Weapons skill, you can perform an attack with two weapons. Each weapon must have a keyword of [Small]. You can attack two opponents with one weapon each, or both weapons against one enemy.

You can combine ranged and melee weapons with these attacks. Your fists each count as a small weapon and you may perform two unarmed attacks in a round.

Inventory

Your journey through the world, while dangerous, is likely to be a lucrative experience. You will amass wealth, trinkets, weapons, and other useful items that might assist you in your future quests or may merely be a treasure to sell.

If you are beginning your adventure with this volume, you own no equipment and will only record items on your inventory when instructed to by the book.

It is important that you record any item on your inventory with the exact wording given by the text, including any information in brackets. Certain rules, especially combat or magic-related items, rely on this information to function correctly in the story. The text may ask you if you have a specific item or an item with a particular effect, and missing any of this information will impede your progress.

Certain items may possess complicated features which will be described by additional text, and you should record this after the item's name.

You could also gain assets or make investments that either regularly cost you an amount or provide an income, and these will have a keyword of [Income] or [Expense]. Record these as normal on your inventory and note the value in the Income and Expenses section on your character sheet. The section on **Money** explains this further.

You may remove any item from your inventory at any point, unless the description notes otherwise, and it is permanently lost.

Here are some examples of inventory items:

Greatsword [Large Melee +4] - This is a two-handed melee weapon with a +4 modifier to your Weapons ability. You may not use a shield with this large weapon equipped.

Hand Crossbow [Small Ranged +0] - This is a small, ranged weapon with no modifier to your Weapons ability. You may equip a shield with this weapon.

Staff of Lighting [Large Melee +0] / [Magic. Strike +3. Air] - This staff is a two-handed melee weapon that can be used as a melee weapon with a +0 modifier to your Weapons ability, or a ranged weapon with a magical attack. If the magical attack is used, it is the Strike spell with 3 attack dice, which have the keyword of [Air].

Full Platemail [Heavy Armour +5] - This full suit of heavy armour increases your armour rating by 5 when worn.

Large Metal Shield [Shield. Heavy Armour +4] - This shield increases your armour rating by 2.

Ring of Endurance [Ring. Magic. Max Health +2] - This magical item increases your Max Health ability by 2 and occupies one of your two 'Ring' equipment slots if worn.

Potion of Healing [Consumable. Health +4] - This potion increases your Health by 4 points. A consumable item that must be removed after use.

Footpad Shoes [Feet. Agility +1] - This item of clothing increases your agility ability modifier by 1 point and occupies your 'Feet' equipment slot if worn. They are not magical, even with the improvement to Agility, and are simply well suited for a specific task.

Climbing Boots [Feet. Climbing Skill] - This item gives you the Climbing skill and occupies your 'Feet' equipment slot if worn.

Investment in Capua Gladiator School [Income +10 x 2 dice] - After purchasing gladiators, you receive a regular payment of between 20 and 120 silver denarii by rolling two dice and multiplying the result by 10. See the next page on Money for more details.

Trade Cog [Sea Transport. Expense -20] - Owning this item allows you unlimited travel via the sea at a regular cost of 20 silver denarii.

You may only wear one item of armour with keywords of [Light Armour] or [Heavy Armour], but not [Shield], and equip one item with a keyword of [Shield]. Shields have the [Light Armour] or [Heavy Armour] keywords too. You may not use a shield if you are using a melee or ranged weapon with a keyword of [Large].

For other items of clothing and accessories, you may only have one item equipped in any of the following body locations, apart from rings which you can wear 2. The item will have one of these locations as a keyword. Head, Neck, Arms, Body, Legs, Feet, Ring (maximum of 2).

You may only carry a maximum of 12 additional items in your backpack, including weapons, armour, and clothing not currently equipped, as well as items with a keyword of [Equipment]. You may carry unlimited 'Other Items' without the keywords above. Rings count as Other Items if not worn

You only gain the benefit of an item of clothing or armour if equipped. A weapon only provides a benefit when used in combat. You may change between items of clothing, armour, or weapons at any point, except if there is an ability test or combat in the section that you are reading. You can change weapons and shields in combat by using an action.

Bonuses from multiple equipped items, spells, consumables, or powers do not stack on a single ability. For example, two items that offer a +1 and a +2 bonus to Agility only give you a +2 (i.e. The highest value) rather than a +3 modifier.

Consumables

The consumables section of your inventory is for small, one use items and will be identified with a keyword of [Consumable]. Provisions, potions, and scrolls are common examples.

You may use a consumable on yourself, or any companion/ally, at any point in the adventure unless there is combat in the section you are reading. Using a consumable in combat requires an action to be spent in a combat round.

You may use a consumable prior to making an ability check unless the text informs you otherwise.

When you gain the benefit from a consumable item, remove it from your character sheet.

Money

The main coinage in the Empire is the silver denarii. There are spots on your character sheet to record how many denarii you hold on your person and how much you have deposited in the Imperial Treasury. There is a treasury office in most cities, and these act as banks for you to deposit funds and valuable items safely. It is highly recommended that you use this service, as it is a risky venture carrying valuables around.

Some items you discover on your travels will be interesting but are useful only from their denarii value, for example, a **Small Gold Eagle Statue [50 Denarii]**.

You do not need to add these individually to your inventory and can just add the value to your silver denarii total if you wish. We can assume the character barters with this at an appropriate point. These are 'Other Items' in your inventory otherwise.

You will have the opportunity to store valuables in the future, and it is perfectly acceptable for a collector to note down the exact details of their treasures for this purpose if they wish.

For anything you own that provides an income or incurs an expense, you must total the values you receive or pay in the Income and Expenses section on your character sheet. A positive number means you gain that coin every cycle, and a negative number costs that amount.

On occasions, the text will instruct you to add or remove this value from the amount of wealth you hold in the Treasury. This occurs immediately and is unavoidable.

You can cover any shortfall in money to pay for expenses from the denarii you carry, but this is optional. If you cannot or will not pay in full for an expense either from the treasury or your own purse when it is due, you immediately lose it from your inventory.

You cannot use money or items deposited in the Treasury until you retrieve them from the magical vault linked to via their numerous offices.

Scavenging

There are many lucrative ways to earn money outside of adventuring. The lands are rich in valuable resources that someone with a keen eye and the right tools can exploit. Selling these to a merchant can provide a good income, but those with the right skills and knowledge can improve these resources further and create larger rewards.

When any of the icons in the table below appear under a section number, you can search for a resource of that type. Resources are finite and there must be an unmarked checkbox available against that resource icon to search.

Icon					
Skill (+3 modifier)	Foraging	Hunting	Mining	Treasure Seeking	Trinket Gathering
Item Required	None	Knife or Dagger	Pickaxe	None	None
Resource Gained	Herbs	Hides	Ore	Denarii	Components
0	Common +1	Common +1	None	None	None
1	Common +2	Common +2	Common +1	30 Denarii	Common +1
2	Common +1 Uncommon +1	Common +3	Common +2	75 Denarii	Common +2
3-4	Uncommon +2	Uncommon +1	Uncommon +1	150 Denarii	Common +1 Uncommon +1
5-6	Uncommon +1 Rare +1	Uncommon +2	Uncommon +2	300 Denarii	Uncommon +2
7+	Rare +2	Rare +1	Uncommon +1 Rare +1	500 Denarii	Uncommon +1 Rare +1

(Number of Successes — row labels 0, 1, 2, 3-4, 5-6, 7+)

Hunting and mining require certain items of equipment in your inventory. If you lack an item with this name for that search, you may not scavenge.

To search an area, add 1 marker to the time track. Mark one box as complete against the icon and make a check against your Scavenging ability. Add a modifier of +3 if you have the relevant skill for that particular environment search.

You may scavenge even if you do not have the related skill.

Each roll of 4+ is a success. If you have a modified level of 0 in your Scavenging ability, roll one die and record one success on a roll of 5+.

Total the number of successes and consult the table above for the resources you find. Add these to the Resources section of your character sheet.

For Treasure, you find items and money to the value of the denarii recorded in the table.

Resting

Resting provides advantages to your character and any companion where the tent symbol below is under the section number you are reading.

You may pause your adventures here and enjoy a **Full Rest**. If you do so, apply the following benefits to your character and companion if you have one.

Add 2 markers to the time track, and mark this chapter's rest complete (the checkbox is at the right of the track).

Restore Health and Prayers to their maximum values.

Gain the **Well Rested [Any Ability +1]** power. The next 3 ability checks, including primary abilities, gain a +1 modifier.

You may spend ability points on improving secondary abilities.

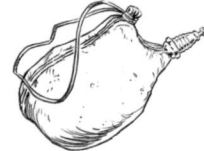

In an emergency, and only if your Health is below 10 points, you may make a **Short Rest** where you see this campfire symbol beneath the section number.

This is a **Short Rest** and represents a relatively safe area for you to tend to your wounds.

If you take a short rest, add 1 marker to the time track and mark this chapter's rest complete.

Raise your Health to 10 points and increase your Prayers by 1 for each level of your Lore ability.

A character with the Survival skill raises their Health to 14 rather than 10 with a short rest.

A companion heals by half of their Max Health, rounding fractions down. Prayers are restored by 1 for each level of their Lore ability.

You may only make one rest of any type per chapter in this volume, and you may not carry forward unused rests to future chapters.

Conditions, Powers, and Unique Masteries

Adventuring is hard and unforgiving, and Health is but one measure of well-being. Acute and chronic conditions last much longer and can reduce your character's effectiveness even with resting and healing.

Time, in many instances, offers the best method for recovery. Unfortunately, some require specialist and often expensive aid.

In contrast, favourable circumstances provide benefits to a character such as enjoying a long and peaceful rest, receiving a priest's blessing, or drinking a useful potion. These positive effects are called powers and are otherwise identical to conditions.

The text will inform you of the effects of any powers and conditions, and the requirements for their removal if permanent. **If non-permanent, they will expire at the end of the current chapter or when you leave the volume you gained them.**

The text may also ask if you have a specific power to perform a certain action, such as **Flight**. This is true if you have currently recorded it in the Powers section, or if you can gain it now from another source, such as a magic item. It is also true if you use an instantaneous power that is used immediately, and not recorded on the character sheet.

If you have an item, spell, or consumable that grants a power, use it at any point to gain that power. You may not use this in a section where combat occurs, and you need to use a combat action to gain the benefit.

If the section has an Ability check, you will be informed if you can use a power, or use an item to gain one, to assist in the check.

Unique masteries are rare and special powers that you may be fortunate enough to learn, or be gifted with in your adventures. The text will provide more information at that time.

The Time Track

Progress of time within these volumes is marked in chapters. Each chapter contain steps which represent an abstract length of time, tracking the story rather than a defined number of hours or days.

When the book instructs you to add markers to the time track, put a cross for each on your character sheet in the leftmost available step of the current chapter. A chapter is completed when all steps are marked on that line.

Some steps on the time track have section numbers beneath them. When you mark that time track step, make a note of the section you are currently on and immediately turn to the section number under the box you have crossed off. Resolve anything in that section before returning to continue your adventure.

If the book instructs you to add markers that will take you beyond one or more section number, resolve each in turn before continuing to the next.

Ignore other letters or symbols under these tracks. These will be revealed later.

If you move to another volume in the series, keep the current time track in this one and resume it once you return.

Marking Your Progress - Codewords and Checkboxes

This game system uses several methods to mark your progress, and your decisions can have far-reaching consequences that may only become fully known much later in your adventures.

When the text instructs you to add a codeword, mark the checkbox next to it on your character sheet. If that codeword is already marked, then do nothing.

When the text asks if you have a codeword, this is true if it is marked as above.

If the text instructs you to remove a codeword, uncheck or erase the marker.

This series extends over many volumes, and you can travel between these as you please. A requirement for a codeword from another book is indicated by a volume number. If the volume number is missing, the codeword is from this book.

Some sections contain checkboxes within the text itself to help record your progress, and the text will inform you how to use these as needed.

Marking your Progress – The Journal

The entire series of *Book of Legends: The Eternal Empire* contains hundreds of plots, quests, and campaigns, some of which span the length of several volumes.

There is a part of your character sheet for your journal into which you should record entries to remind you of where you are in your adventures.

Some segments within these volumes will instruct you to add a line to your journal, and this becomes an active journal entry.

As with items in your inventory, it is important you record these accurately, especially the journal entry number at the start of the name, as these are used to track your progress in your many quests and tasks within the story.

A journal entry might require several success markers before the task is complete. This is noted at the end of the journal entry name with multiple values, x5 or x10, for example.

No value means there is just one requirement to complete the journal entry.

In the example below, you have killed 5 rats for journal entry #521 in Roma, Volume V. This is an active and incomplete entry.

Entry 521 - Kill rats in the city sewers (Roma - V) x10 ✓ ✓ ✓ ✓ ✓

Once you kill another 5 rats, you will have 10 ticks and the entry's requirements will be met. This becomes an active and complete journal entry. The player can return to the quest giver to receive their reward.

When you receive your reward for completing the entry, the text will instruct you to remove the entry from your journal. This entry then becomes inactive.

When you explore the lands of the Eternal Empire and beyond, some areas only become available when you have a specific entry active. This means one of the many paths, roads, or areas that you encounter only becomes of interest when you need to use them.

At the foot of a section, you will be presented with a number in an open book. If this entry in your journal is active **and incomplete**, you may turn to the section number if you want to begin that task.

If not, ignore it and continue on your way.

521 Turn to **400**.☐ Complete

The option to continue with this task is at the end of the section, and you must resolve all instructions in the section before choosing that option.

When you complete these journal entries, you will frequently find yourself back at the starting point for those tasks. The text will remind you to check the box next to the journal icon on your return and this task is thus no longer available in future.

Companions

During your travels, you will encounter a variety of interesting and skilled people. You may persuade some of these to join you in your travels.

You will predominantly recruit a companion to aid you in combat or to provide certain skills that your character may not possess, for example, the ability to pick locks. They remain in the background in most encounters, and do not make any ability checks for them unless the text states otherwise.

The text will specify if a companion's skill can be used if you do not possess it.

A companion will aid you in any way you see fit during combat and you will have full control of how they use any special skills, spells, and prayers against enemies. You may order them to remain out of combat if you desire.

They will not always use their powers to aid your character directly, for example healing, but information on their behaviour is on their character sheet at the back of the volume in which you encountered them. They will never give you items or money they own from their inventory.

If a companion's Health is 3 or less, they will not join you in combat. If their Health drops below 3 during combat, and this is not healed to 4 or more, they will use their action to flee combat, but only if the text offers the option to flee. Otherwise, they are forced to remain in combat with you.

You may use a companion to carry equipment that you might otherwise not be able to carry yourself, such as magic crystals, if you hold the maximum of 50. This equipment is yours and can be used as you see fit.

If a companion dies in combat, make a note of the section you are currently on, and turn to the relevant section number in the volume you recruited them. Details of that section are on the companion's character sheet at the end of that volume.

You may only have one companion accompany you at one time. If you recruit another, or wish to part ways with your current companion, remove their details from your character sheet. Record any changes to their inventory in the space provided on their page at the back of this volume. They will usually return to where you originally met, and you may employ their services again in future.

Unless the text states otherwise, a companion will not move between volumes. As soon as you leave one volume for another, a companion will depart your service in the same way if you had recruited another.

Companions may join you for a fee. You pay them in the same manner as other expenses from the Imperial Treasury. If you do not have enough denarii in the Treasury or on your person when you need to pay their fee, they will promptly leave your service.

Copy the companion's information from the back of the volume they are recruited over to your character sheet.

Magic

Spells

Any character with at least level 1 in their Mystical ability has knowledge of the use of crystal magic. Following the Divine Fire, crystals scattered over the lands in the fireball's path, from the isle of Britannia through to its eventual impact in Sicilia.

These crystals, when combined with the correct words and actions, provide a wealth of powerful effects to the user. These spells below are split into combat spells and status buffs.

Unique spells, recorded on your character sheet under the Unique Masteries, have their own rules recorded in their descriptions. There are five common colours of crystal, each representing five elements: Green [Earth], blue [Water], clear [Air], red [Fire] and purple [Aether].

The first four crystals create obvious effects reflecting their element. Attacks with fire burn, staggering an opponent with an air crystal could be a violent gust of wind or a lightning strike throwing them backwards. An attack with water can be ice or frost, and protection with earth providing a hard skin of rock, for example.

These effects are individual to the user, and it is not uncommon to see magic users casting the same strike spell with earth crystals, and one caster raining boulders on their enemies, with another shooting granite shards from their outstretched hands.

Aether crystals are rarer and have only recently been discovered in the past century during expeditions into the dark lands of Sicilia. Their power is at the same strength as other crystals but lack a physical substance not visible when casting. The horrific effects on the target can be seen, with some poor unfortunates vanishing in a cloud of dust or reduced to mindless and gibbering wrecks.

Only the five crystals mentioned above may be used for magic. Crystal of other colours may only be used if the text states so.

There are whispers that expert users with a fine understanding of aether crystals can command further strange and fantastical effects, but no one has observed proof of such power.

You may carry a maximum of 50 crystals, of all colours, at one time because of the strength of their energies. Attempting to move more simultaneously has proved fatal to all attempting it, no matter their level of aptitude.

Combat Spells

These spells, as the name suggests, are used during combat or to prepare for combat. The effects are identical irrespective of what type of crystal is used. However, some foes are resistant, immune, or have weaknesses to certain effects. All spells have the keyword of [Magic] plus the keyword of the crystal used.

In a combat round, you may cast one of the following spells as your action. You may only use crystals of a single type for each attempt, and you can only use a number that is equal to or lower than your Mystical ability for each action.

Unique spells, listed as combat spells, can also be cast as an action at this point.

Astral Warrior	Creates a spectral warrior identical in looks to the caster but clad in ornate armour and wielding a large two-handed weapon of the caster's choice. Each crystal used gives this warrior a Weapons ability of 1, and Health of 2.
	This warrior is considered an ally in combat for its actions and the bonus gained from the Tactics skill. Because of its heavy armour and weapon, it will be the primary target for opponents.
	Any damage inflicted on the warrior in combat has the keyword of the crystal used to create it. It is resistant to damage received with that keyword, halving that damage (rounding down). It disappears after all foes are defeated or if the caster dies.
Healing	For each crystal used, add 3 points to the Health of yourself or a companion. Health cannot exceed its maximum value in this way. Healing may also be freely cast outside combat at the same cost.
Protection	For each crystal used, add 1 point to the armour rating for yourself, a companion or an ally. This lasts until the entire combat encounter ends. Gain resistance to damage with the crystals' keyword, halving damage received (rounding down).
Speed	Requires Mystical level 2 or above. You may use 2 crystals to give yourself or an ally two actions in this combat round in addition to the one used casting this spell.

This spell uses no action and once cast, the character or companion may continue with their first action straight after. You may take the additional second action at any point before the enemies' actions begin.

This spell may only be cast once per combat round.

Stagger	Remove one crystal to cause one enemy to stagger back from combat. The caster's Mystical ability must be equal to or higher than the enemy's Weapons ability and the enemy cannot attack for 3 combat rounds.

The enemy spends this time steadying themselves to rejoin the fray and will not use attacks or abilities against the character or allies. If you attack that individual, they will immediately return to combat and will continue to fight normally in that round.

Usually, a maximum number of enemies can be engaged in melee combat with a friendly combatant. A staggered enemy remains in melee combat, and counts towards this total, as they fumble and obstruct their allies.

Strike	Make a ranged combat attack on one opponent as detailed in the combat section. Each crystal used gives 2 attack dice with a 4+ required to hit successfully.

The attack has the keyword of the crystal used.

Status Buffs

Buffs are spells that temporarily increase a score when making a secondary ability check. For each level of Mystical ability your character has, and before any dice are rolled, they may use one crystal of any colour to add 1 level to the ability check and gain 1 extra die per crystal spent. The modified level of that ability can exceed level 5 in this manner.

A Character may use a maximum of 1 crystal per level of their Mystical ability per casting attempt. A status buff cannot increase the primary abilities of Lore, Mystical, or Weapons unless the text states otherwise.

As the bonus from a status buff improves the level of the ability, it is applied in addition to any modifiers currently in effect.

Magical Items

Some items possess magical effects that are usable by anyone, even with no Mystical or Lore ability. These may have passive effects and will increase (or if you are unlucky and it is cursed, decrease) abilities, or they could be combat focused and useful only when fighting.

An item with a [Magic] keyword has a magical effect, and is described further within the same bracket. An item with [Magic. Strike +5. Fire] can make a single Strike attack (see the previous page) with 5 dice and the keyword of [Fire].

Magical items will usually have a limited number of uses, and the description will detail how many charges it has available. Each use of that power reduces the charge by 1, and when this value reaches zero, you cannot use the powers until you recharge the item.

The power of some magical items will be unknown when first encountered. They will have the section number and volume to turn to if you have or gain the Magical Sense skill, or if you employ the services of someone with that skill.

You may only make one attempt at identifying a magic item with the Magical Sense skill.

Prayers

Using prayers is like that of spells. Each level of Lore that a character has achieved provides 6 Prayers that allow them to modify ability checks.

By using a Prayer, a character may add or subtract 1 from the value of any die after it has been rolled. This includes when attacking, either with their Weapons or Mystical abilities, when making an ability check, or changing an enemy's attack dice.

Points can be split among different dice if required. For example, you receive two damaging hits on the character of a 6 and 4 by an enemy. You can reduce this to no hits by using 4 Prayers, reducing both dice to 3.

You can use a maximum of 1 Prayer per level of Lore you have in a single combat round, ability check, or other circumstances where dice are used. In the above example, a character would need at least level 4 in Lore to reduce the damage to zero.

Using a Prayer to adjust a die by at least one point gives that die your deity's keyword. Thus, an attacking roll, whether it was originally damaging or not, could be turned into a more powerful one that takes advantage of an enemy's weakness. An enemy's attack could also be rendered less powerful or even ineffective if your character becomes resistant or immune to a certain keyword from that attack.

Prayers are regained by resting, and other opportunities will be available during your adventures to restore them.

The Birth of the Eternal Empire

The Divine Fire: AUC 830

It was early on a warm March evening in the seventh year of the benign rule of Emperor Titus Flavius Vespasianus, 77AD in our modern calendar, and 830 years after the founding of Rome.

From the north, a blinding light more brilliant than a hundred suns streaked a fiery trail across the dusky yellow sky.

Racing at considerable speed over the western coast of Italia towards the southern provinces, it left an arced trail of black smoke and dust in its wake as it disappeared over the horizon in a matter of a few brief seconds.

The southern sky then glowed a warm, bright orange as if the land of the Empire itself burned, before fading into the muted dusk that once peacefully marked the hour.

The sun had disappeared below the horizon when the thunder arrived. A single terrible crash as a blow from Vulcan's hammer might strike his earthly anvil. At that instant, pottery, and glass turned into deadly airborne shards with larger objects, even citizens, hurled about by the invisible and destructive force.

The priests offered many sacrifices to their gods over the next months as terrible stories emerged of the apocalyptic events. Graphic tales from survivors spoke of the intensity of the inferno. A heat of such magnitude, it vaporised people, trees, and even stone buildings, in the devastated island province of Sicilia.

Those who were not instantly turned to dust, but were close enough for the wall of searing fire, wore charred and blistered skin for the remainder of their brief lives, while others slowly suffocated from the creeping black soot.

Further out, the stories were not wholly gruesome tales of death. Numerous and miraculous incidents of survivors emerged that had escaped the worst of the conflagration. Indeed, it soon appeared only a tenth of the island had suffered from this destruction, and most people survived the initial blast.

Many of these survivors would, in time, regret their apparent good fortune as the Fire's effects continued for generations.

The Children of Light: AUC 832-835

From the frontiers of the province of Britannia to the burnt landscape of Sicilia, incidents of children born with mutations became commonplace. The frequency was most prominent in lands over which the Fire had travelled, with distrust and suspicion escalating all the way to outright violence, following these births.

Out of fear, neighbours and friends forced families to escape to remote areas or even abandon their children to the elements or animals.

Some mutations were, as years passed, discovered to be quite benign and offered the affected children many benefits. It took decades, but the empire eventually accepted these new people as citizens.

Many thousands of unique individuals, races, and distinct species drew breath during this time, but most bloodlines soon disappeared with the sterility inherent in many mutations.

Violence at the hands of others was another common cause of extinction. Even suffering these challenges, several races and species branched from humanity and not only survived, but thrived.

The richly hued, blue-skinned peregrine altas found a home within the great cities of the Roman Empire, ascending the levels of power effortlessly through their vast intellect and charisma.

Their smaller cousins, the peregrine agilia, were happy to live in both cities and rural locations, and they became a common sight across the lands. Both altas and agilia are now completely separate species from humans, and no cross-species procreation has ever come to term.

The rock-skinned durum flocked together and lived as far as they could from centres of populations. Their hardy physique and temperament allows them to thrive in cold, hostile environments such as the northern borders with the Riye One Kingdom, and mountainous regions of the world where they thrive in semi-independent states.

Terra volatis were the last dominant race to flourish. They spread themselves as widely as the agilia across the lands and are seen in most areas of the world. Their numbers are lower than other races, and most are solitary individuals interacting with others only when necessary.

The Children of Darkness: AUC 830-835

While many under the fire's path of 830 did not suffer any ill effects either themselves or with their unborn children, those that were affected could live with their differences to a degree

However, some were not so fortunate. Adults and children in parts of Sicilia scarcely escaped with their lives, and those who persevered emerged horribly disfigured, wracked with blistering pain. Avoiding the daylight, they only emerge to hunt other survivors, craving their flesh as if it was an opiate.

Others, further away from the blast, birthed similar mutations to their more fortunate cousins, but with it also suffered horrific ill effects. These afflictions, along with banishment from normal society, enraged the new creatures, and it took just a few generations for them to become bloodthirsty monsters whose sole aim was to destroy the Empire and every other creature living within.

The Wall: AUC 840

Other life changed with the fire's power as animals and humans did. Trees, plants, mosses, and vines grew at an astonishing rate over the continent, turning it into almost one single lush green forest.

Tracing the line over which the fireball took on its devastating journey, the growth was at its greatest. Thick trees grew strong and tall, reaching high into the clouds for over a thousand feet across the western borders of Britannia and Hibernia, and rending the province of Gallia in half.

Traversal of the impenetrable wall was out of the question. The thick branches and dense foliage made progress slow on the outer edges, but impossible at the centre. Some reports spoke of aggressive plants, attacking and consuming hapless explorers, which further lessened the will to find passage.

Now, the only method to reach the western provinces in Europe without sea travel is a deep tunnel that links Lugdunum in Gallia Occidentis, and Porta Gallia in the northern

Alps. A daily scouring is still required to hold at bay the fast root growth that would block the tunnel within weeks if left unchecked.

The Eternal Empire: AUC 868

Emperor Trajan's untimely death in 868 created a power vacuum that saw one of the most fraught moments in Imperial history. The great families fought for the approval of the senate and administrators, and all provinces sent delegates to ensure they were represented.

Out of the chaos stepped a peregrine alta. He was improbably tall, taller than even the loftiest alta, towering high above any who had lived before. His skin was a much darker blue than his brethrens' with deep purple shadows creating a stark, two-tone effect. Well-educated and intelligent, as was standard for many others descended from that branch of the Children of Light, his tar black eyes appeared infinite in their depth.

He was known only as Caius, and through a vast amount of effort over the summer months, he made promises and threats in equal measures to ensure they offered him the opportunity to rule.

Allaying the suspicions of the ordinary people was not so straightforward, and along with coordinated efforts by other candidates to halt his rise, the Imperial crown appeared but a dream for him.

A general of the Praetorian Guard by the name of Proculus was not willing to allow this slight prospect to remain even a dream. Deciding this mutant would not approach any closer to the throne, he and several officers planned a public show of imperial force against this monster.

Heavily armoured guards interrupted a speech by Caius in the Forum of Roma on the first day of September.

They surrounded Caius, and the general announced to the sizeable crowd that no mutant would rule the Empire. Some cheered and others gasped in shock as the guards and officers surrounded the surprised alta. Two officers then forced Caius to his knees as Proculus, with no hesitation, brought his sword down hard on the back of his neck.

It bounced harmlessly off.

The Praetorian Guards, momentarily wrong-footed by this surprise, then stabbed the kneeling Caius hard with their spears, but these were also to no effect, the blade hitting an invisible barrier an inch from the kneeling alta's clothing and skin. Throughout the next few moments, Caius rose from his knees and raised his hands to the astonished crowd, even as he was repeatedly struck with the guards' impotent blows.

Proculus and his guards began slowing from the efforts, no surprise as they wore full armour and were striking hard. They then stiffened further until, eventually, they were wholly immobile and frozen in their stances.

The apparent invulnerability of Caius, along with his power to freeze the attackers in place, was demonstration enough of his might for the crowd. The senate was convinced by those self-same reasons, and on the ides of September, thirteen days later, Caius Quirinius Romulus ascended the imperial throne.

His first action as emperor was to have the traitor general and his guards carried to the palace at Palatine Hill. They remained frozen in the original positions from their attempt on Caius' life.

"I am Caius Quirinius Romulus, Defender of the Empire. I am your emperor." he stood tall, speaking with confidence to the crowd.

"Behold the dawning of a new era of peace and prosperity."

The guards were the first to regain control of their bodies. Most threw themselves at his mercy and, to the surprise of many, earned a full pardon. Whether Emperor Romulus, as he was soon to be installed, wished to show the crowd the extent of his mercy is unknown. Some say he understood the need for the emperor's personal guards to follow all orders without question.

One guard, however, was more defiant and screamed, "Mutant Emperor! Mutant Empire!"

This screaming and spitting continued as the guards dragged him to Traitor's Gate, as it was henceforth named. This gatehouse, at the northern side of the Imperial Palace complex overlooking the Forum, had a sheer drop of over 150 feet to the bottom of the Palatine hill from the towers.

The traitor guard's broken body was left as a warning at the foot of the eastern tower, where the rusted and dented armour remains untouched in the modern-day city.

General Proculus was not fortunate enough to receive the option to repent or receive a quick death. Indeed, any death might have been preferable.

His statuesque form stands today as a warning at the vast Praetorian Guard Barracks to the northeast of the Forum. It is not known whether the General is still conscious or aware of his surroundings in this state. Claims the perfectly preserved form has gradually shifted over the years cannot be corroborated as no images created over that time survive.

1 Martius IA1

Half a year of celebrations followed the investiture of Emperor Romulus, and 1 March AUC 869 was renamed the first day of the first year of the Imperium Aeternum. The Eternal Empire.

As the years and centuries passed, the Empire grew, flourishing under the firm but fair hand of the immortal Emperor Romulus. Cities grew into thriving metropolises and the people were happy. However, the dark taint of those who had not been as fortunate during the Divine Fire remained, and as time passed, they became bolder and more violent towards their flourishing neighbours.

With ferocious speed, the villages fell and were soon followed by the unprotected towns. Now, the only real safety is secured from the walled cities and larger towns, and travel is conducted with haste along the dangerous highways of the Empire.

To begin your adventure, turn to section **1**.

Book of Legends: The Eternal Empire

Volume 0 - Prologue

Chapter I

A Time for Legends: 17 Februarius IA1099

Today

Creaking timbers of the ship that has been your home for the past weeks bring soothing familiarity as you stir from a deep slumber in your comfortable bunk. The intermittent storms that wracked the ship overnight have subsided, and all is calm.

The morning air is warm and fresh, yet with it a strange scent lingers. A faint sooty aroma laced with an acrid tinge. Not burning food, not wood, something unnatural and chemical. You open your eyes and rub the dust from them, squinting as daggers of sunlight lance through the gaps in the deck timbers.

Distant shouts from the deck below cause you to lift your head to hear the commotion more clearly, and as you do, the deafening roar of cannons explodes into life.

You fall gracelessly from your bunk and scramble to collect your belongings. You are not too quick either as a cannonball rips open a jagged hole in the ship's hull next to where you were soundly asleep just a few moments ago.

The mattress protects you from the worst of the shrapnel, but you still feel the sharp sting of several splinters driven into unprotected areas of your flesh.

Clambering up the slippery wooden stairs to the main deck, you squint again as your eyes adjust to the bright morning sun. In the distance, a matter of several miles away, you see a dark land with a pillar of black and purple smoke rising into the blue skies.

Sicilia. The land of death where the Divine Fire struck over a thousand years ago. The column marks the unstoppable conflagration from the star that formed it, burning without end ever since. Imperial edicts have decreed the land strictly off limits, on penalty of a long and painful death.

This is especially worrying to you as your ship is now certainly within the exclusion zone.

To the port side, three well-armed and armoured battleships from the Empire's central fleet of the Grand Navy, advance with a following wind at immense speed. From the nearest vessel, a salvo of shots again rips into the tortured hull of your transport, and it tilts towards the aggressors.

You should have paid more care than employ a cheap smuggler for passage across the seas, but your self-criticism is too late.

The captain, an old and occasional acquaintance from your homeland, was the cheapest option for travel and he just needed to make "one quick stop" on your way. It was all you could afford, but now the price has increased in blood.

Men scream as they fall from the vessel and corpses litter the water. The ship lists heavily, its contents ejected into the dark blue sea. A sea that you can observe now hosts other beings. Hungry beings.

You wait, crouched on the deck, then clinging to the side of the ship before it eventually slips beneath the waves. The screams of sailors as they are eaten alive by the denizens of the sea fill your ears and the waters consume you.

Most possessions, little that you had, are lost to the sea, but you keep two crucially important items: your brigandine and dagger.

Add **Dagger [Small Melee +0]** and **Leather Brigandine [Light Armour +1]** to your inventory.

Turn to **76**.

2

You approach a pair of heavy and weather-beaten boulders partially obstructing your progress along the rocky path. On the nearest edge, small scraps of bone and leather lay scattered on the trail, the remains of a poor unfortunate whose travels ended here.

You roll the larger pieces around with your boots, but nothing of interest is revealed. Glancing around, the area is otherwise quiet.

To go west towards the coast, turn to **85**. To continue east, ascending the mountain, turn to **133**.

3

You turn a familiar corner of the track and see the red tent of the old couple, who sit outside as you had first met them, a pot of stew bubbling away. They look up with smiles beaming across their faces.

It takes but a few moments for them to recognise you and, as they realise who you are, their kind expressions turn to a twisted burst of vicious, snarling laughter.

"Sit down!" the woman screeches, her tone is uncomfortably high, bringing discomfort and pain to your ears.

"You look tired." her companion hisses as he stands, his face contorted in a hateful sneer.

Their eyes glow bright green as the mocking and then screaming intensifies. You feel somewhat nauseous and light-headed at this unnatural assault on your senses, and you continue along the path at a brisk pace.

These creatures do not follow, nor attempt to stop your escape, and you leave the area with no further effects.

To travel northwest towards a crossroads, turn to **59**. To go southeast to a Y junction, turn to **198**.

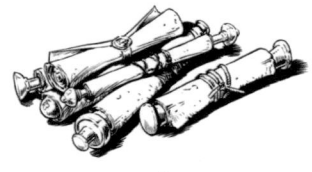

4

The treacherous conditions on the path combined with the low light cause you to stagger and your feet dislodge a large stone. Your ankle twists at an unnatural angle and the sudden jolt of pain sends you plummeting down the side of the hill, with dirt and rocks following you like a wave. Your head cracks hard against a protruding rock at the base, and you collapse in a bloodied heap.

The sudden events take you completely by surprise and you cannot react with any ability, spell, or power.

Lose 3 points of Health.

To continue east, turn to **190**. To travel west, turn to **88**.

5

Your journey through the open brush is uneventful, yet it surprises you to see the smoke that envelops the island ends sharply at this northernmost tip.

The contrast is unnaturally abrupt and appears as if a magical barrier, as straight as a building's facade, protects this headland from the wall of smoke that plunges the southern portion of the island into darkness.

To go north to the tip of the headland, turn to **50**. To head south to the farm, turn to **141**.

6

The narrow trail that crosses the south-westerly edge of the island hugs the coastline on its meandering journey. Within a few feet on one side are the deep blue Mediterranean waters, and on the other are the high brown, yellow, and white cliffs that block your direct passage to the central region of the land.

If you have already marked the checkbox below against the current chapter, turn to **93**.

Otherwise, mark the checkbox below against the current chapter and turn to that section number.

Chapter I, turn to **191**. ☐

Chapter II, turn to **175**. ☐

Chapter III, turn to **52**. ☐

7

If you have the codeword **HALVE**, turn to **139**.

Otherwise, turn to **92**.

8

The treacherous, steep trail links the eastern coast to the tall peaks of the central domain of the island. The going is difficult, and you must slow to a crawl in several places, especially where the ground is near vertical. However, the old path is well-preserved and with care, you traverse the route without incident.

To head southeast, descending to the coast, turn to **190**. To proceed northwest through dense green jungle, turn to **82**.

9

You have passed along this stretch before and with that experience, can avoid the dangers that it presents. Your progress is uneventful along the trail on this occasion.

To continue north, turn to **100**. To resume your journey south, turn to **143**.

10

The wood's dark green interior stifles the atmosphere with its oppressive gloom, an unwelcoming environment to you or any other creature. The wind funnels hard through this area and continues to chill your bones with a high-pitched, off-tone whistle. Thankfully, the sounds are purely natural this time and lack the pained screaming you had experienced before.

Proceeding onwards, the clearing holds the fresh bodies of the unfortunate hosts you defeated earlier, lying lifeless where they fell. The corpses, untouched by hungry wildlife, are an indictment of the power of the unnatural organism that once stood proud here, and which now remains a lifeless grey hulk.

To leave the clearing and head north, turn to **146**. To go south, turn to **198**.

11

If you have the codeword **DEITY**, turn to **104**.

The pathway is narrow, rising and falling under a thick jungle canopy. A thick bed of rotten wet leaves covers the wiry grass and soft mud underfoot, and dense, vibrant green foliage that once only existed in lands far from here, encloses it on each side.

You did not notice on your approach, but where the edge of the canopy opens to the sky, a sharp crackling fills the air. Akin to lighting, it has a tinny and hollow echo that closely surrounds you.

A deep rumbling shakes the ground and your hair prickles in the warm, charged air. It strengthens with each moment.

The exact source of this atmospheric phenomenon is unknown to you, yet it screams immediate peril.

You may abandon your progress and return the way you came if you so wish. Westwards, you view the ruins of a village in the distance. To the east, the apex of a ruined temple peeks above the treeline.

If you wish to go back west, turn to **34**. To return east, turn to **82**.

If you want to continue ahead, and if you have already marked the box below against the current chapter, turn to **58**.

Otherwise, mark the checkbox below against the current chapter and turn to that section number.

Chapter I, turn to **127**. ☐

Chapter II, turn to **193**. ☐

Chapter III, turn to **148**. ☐

12

Your decision not to destroy the heart took some moments to consider. Your decision to retreat from the wood is expedited by the three animated hosts as they rise to their feet and lumber towards you once more.

To exit the clearing north, turn to **146**. To travel south turn to **198**.

13

As you progress towards your destination, you detect a barely audible sound of squawking high in the distance. You crane your head upwards, scanning the sky yet see no life.

This is not unusual you have discovered in your brief sojourn on this island, as many inhabitants are excessively vocal due to the numerous and convenient hiding spots. They are also rather difficult to observe for this exact reason.

You take a slight pause and use this time to admire the central peak's majestic west face as it rises into the sky. From this angle, the summit looks to overhang the path like a claw.

The sounds continue to approach and intensify in their urgency but quieten after a short time, the sources never revealed.

To travel north towards the peak, turn to **85**. To go south, turn to **100**.

14

The forest surrounding the path you now tread is bright and lush, almost tropical in its vibrance. Closely bordering the path, the thick foliage makes deeper exploration impossible, but your progress down the trail is one you manage with ease.

Ahead, supporting a ruined pediment, you glimpse white columns towering above breaks in the forest canopy, and from the same direction, the unmistakable crashing sounds of combat.

You approach with caution as the battle rages. Shouts with several voices, and screeches from creatures whose species you cannot yet determine, cut through the air. Progressing forward, the trees open into a large clearing where you see the marble pillars form part of an ancient, ruined temple.

Ahead, the bloodied and broken body of an Imperial legionary lies face down on the cobblestones next to the corpse of a giant beetle. A centurion faces off against another, which rears high for an attack, its bright orange carapace shining brilliantly in the light.

A third beetle emerges from the treeline close to your position and lunges towards a peregrine alta grasping a long spear. His other hand cackles with fierce electric power, the blue skin of his arm shining almost pure white with the energy.

The first beetle slams down hard on the centurion, one of its mandibles thrust into her exposed neck, and she collapses to the floor. Her lifeblood runs over the steps of the temple, turning stone, grass, and dirt a dark, shining red.

Both beetles now turn their attention to the lone alta, who lets forth a sizzling electric blue lance from his palm that singes the thick carapace of the nearest creature.

If you want to aid the peregrine alta and fight these monstrous creatures, turn to **48**.

To avoid the fight and either sneak around or return on the path you arrived, turn to **176**.

15

The stew is thick and the venison tender after hours of gentle cooking. Carrots and peas add colour and texture to the spicy brown broth, and you eagerly devour the delicious, rustic fare. Mopping up the remains with a soft flatbread, you recline in your seat, content from your first hot meal in a while.

Add **Blessing of Somnus [Max Health +1]** to the Powers section of your character sheet. This is a cumulative effect. If you have already received this blessing, amend the description to +2 or +3 as appropriate.

This power increases both your Max Health and Health by 1 point. Also apply this to your companion if you have one.

You spy a longbow within the tent laid upon the bed and you enquire about hunting on the island.

"You must be so quiet here. Many dangers which spook the animals," the lady explains. "The wildlife is plentiful and diverse, and we eat well."

You agree. They clearly do not go without.

After you have all finished your bowls, the man retrieves a tall, clear bottle of red liquid from a crate. He then produces three silver goblets from a small wooden display box, fills one, and offers it to you.

"How about some wine?" he asks with a smile.

If you accept, turn to **97**. If you do not accept, turn to **40**.

16

Remove **60 Denarii** from your inventory.

Add the codeword **FEAST**.

The boy takes the money with a grin and nods. "I'll make sure you get to where you need to go." He then slips away, a confident energy and spring to his steps.

Turn to **147**.

17

Add 1 marker to the time track and if this takes you to the end of Chapter III, turn to section **91** instead of **101**.

If you have the codeword **DEITY**, turn to **114**.

If you have the codeword **KNAVE**, turn to **159**.

You crawl on your front to a high vantage point above the most southerly bay on the island. Remains of buildings in what formerly was a small harbour town surround the bay. The stone dockside is intact and in good condition, with one wooden jetty in use.

About a dozen rough-looking men and women of various species go about their business, either sitting, chatting and drinking, or moving crates and barrels into several of the still-standing buildings. You spot a small rowing boat leaving the bay and on board, you make out several figures.

A line of slaves sits chained by the hands and feet with one ruffian keeping watch over them. They are pirates and judging by the quality of their equipment, they are rather successful ones at that. They appear fresh and in good spirits and you surmise they have only just arrived in the bay, maybe relieving their comrades whom you can see leaving in the distant boat.

A quick count of the number of opponents, at least 12 fresh, well-equipped, and skilled fighters, you estimate that any fight would likely end in your death.

There is a small vessel, large enough for several dozen crates and at least 15 passengers, moored at the end of one dock. If you could sneak to it, you could stow away and leave the island. It is small for a seagoing vessel and is likely just a transport boat to their main vessel, no doubt anchored off the island elsewhere.

You could also take the brazen approach and just walk up to them. How hard could it be to persuade them to let you join them until you reach civilisation?

This location is challenging and will require delicate and careful progress, else any mistake could lead to fatal consequences. Any companion that travels with you will thus wait atop the cliffs and rejoin you once you leave the area. They will still assist you in combat when necessary.

To fight the pirates, turn to **65**.

If you would like to sneak onto the boat, turn to **39**.

To talk to them, turn to **195**.

Otherwise, you can slip away unnoticed. To proceed west, turn to **6**. To head north, turn to **88**.

18

Even with good visibility and dry conditions, the rocks and dirt easily come loose, impeding your progress. You stumble on your way, using as much as you can of the sparse grass, rocks, and handholds in the dried dirt to keep yourself from faltering.

This works for some parts, but taking hold of a rock protruding from a steeper section, it easily comes loose with your weight, and you fall back onto a ledge 15 feet below. Small rocks bounce off your prone body and you rise to your feet, battered and sore.

Lose 2 Health. If you have the **Feather** or **Flight** power, or the Reflexes skill, only lose 1 Health as you had a brief time to react and mitigate your decent somewhat.

The fall is so sudden that if you have neither power nor skill, you cannot react in time to gain a benefit from other items or means.

To resume your journey west to the mountain peak, turn to **133**. To continue northeast to the crossroads, turn to **59**.

19

You arrive back to your ship and the crew prepares to cast off. Below is the cost of travel in denarii (d) on a ship you do not own between this island and other provinces in the Eastern Empire.

If you own an item in your inventory with a keyword of [Sea Transport], you pay nothing for this journey.

You must have enough money on your person for this journey, otherwise you must find an alternative method to travel.

Upon leaving the island, increase your Health and Prayers to their maximum values along with any companion's. Remove any effects that expire when you leave a volume.

30d.	Italia. Turn to Volume I, section **994**.
30d.	Roma. Turn to Volume V, section **219**.
65d.	Hispania and Gallia. Turn to Volume II, section **414**.
70d.	Graecia and Byzantium. Turn to Volume VIII, section **393**.
80d.	Africa Proconsularis. Turn to Volume III, section **458**.
150d.	Britannia. Turn to Volume IV, section **731**.
120d.	Aegyptus. Turn to Volume IX, section **885**.
---	Sicilia. Warning, this course of action is highly illegal and you proceed at your own risk. You can only attempt this if you own a vessel with a keyword of [Sea Transport]. Turn to Volume X, section **915**.

To continue exploring the island, turn to **164**.

20

The edge of the farmland is eerily serene, yet it presents you with a scene implying anything but quiet. You note at least one-half of the crops have been destroyed, consumed by an unseen and ravenous force. A force comprising some significant numbers hiding in deep burrows, the entrances from which you count scores of around the fields.

There is no movement within the area of standing crops, and you move through without incident, albeit at a careful and watchful passing.

To travel north to the farm, turn to **141**. To move south to the T junction, turn to **68**.

21

The northernmost point of the island is at a lower elevation to the central mass, and in stark contrast to the rocky ground elsewhere, the soil here is dark and rich with a wide variety of vibrant, colourful crops bursting forth in bloom. In the centre of three small fields is a quaint yellow stone farmhouse with smoke billowing from the tall grey chimney.

The island narrows at this point, with grassland stretching west to east between coasts. The farmhouse, fields, and the gentle seas paint a tranquil vista.

As you approach the building, the calm picture snaps to one of intense threat. Shimmering blue forms of three spectral wolves pace around the house, testing the door and windows, probing for a way to gain entry. You hear the screams of at least two people inside, and focusing on their immediate prey, the ghostly wolves are unaware of your presence.

If you wish to help those inside the farmhouse by fighting these apparitions, turn to **66**.

If you do not wish to assist, a trail leads north towards a headland, the most northerly tip of the island. A path leads south, returning to the wooded and mountainous areas.

To proceed north, turn to **177**. To journey south, turn to **43**.

22

Tying the rope around the base of the tree, you secure it tightly and lower yourself into the inky darkness. Your eyes adjust to the gloom, and you realise the shaft is shallower than you first observed. The rope touches the floor below and you drop deftly the final few feet.

Your eyes adjust further to the darkness, and a faint purple glow bathes you in light from a polished circular mirror set into the grey rock. The disc measures about 3 feet in diameter, and as you approach, you notice it is not a mirror, but a window into a similar cave where exotic plant life radiates an amethyst hue.

The window appears moulded of thick solid glass, and peering closer, you just about make out a symbol of interlinked hexagonal shapes embossed on the surface.

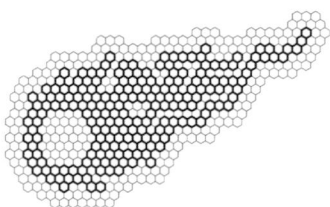

You put your hand to the glass and meet slight resistance before it passes effortlessly through. A hot, tingling sensation causes you to pull back sharply, and you step back to consider your options.

If you advance through the window, turn to Section **420** in Volume X and remove any effects that expire when you leave a volume.

Otherwise, your only other option is to climb back out of the sinkhole, retrieve your rope, and resume exploring the island above ground.

To continue north, turn to **34**. If you would like to resume your travels south, turn to **88**.

23

The low light and previous deluges have caused this route to become a perilous trial of your skill and stamina. Each step on the saturated and unstable ground, then adds to a test of your luck.

Even proceeding with the utmost caution, you still slip on an apparently stable foothold and roll down the steep drop to the base of the mountain, hitting several large protruding rocks in your fall.

Lose 3 Health.

Add 1 marker to the time track.

You lay in agony for what feels like an age before your bruised body is ready for you to stand and continue.

You carefully climb to where you lost your footing. From this point, the solid rocks provide ample hand and footholds and suffer none of the dangers of the slick, muddy path from where you fell. You continue your way without further incident or injury.

To climb west, climbing further to the mountain peak, turn to **133**. To travel northeast to the crossroads, turn to **59**.

24

Add 1 marker to the time track.

If you have the codeword **NOVEL**, turn to **10**. If not, turn to **111**.

25

The rocks, rain, and darkness all conspire to make your progress as difficult as possible. Several times the ground gives way, or the black haze tricks your eyes, and you clumsily stumble on the uneven ground.

Your slow progress is made more tortuous by the horizontal, driving rain. It pummels your face and you struggle to see further than a few feet ahead as you squint in the torrent.

However, your careful actions are not for naught. You persist and a few of these near misses aside, you persevere through the difficult sections.

To journey east, turn to **190**. To head west, turn to **88**.

26

The coastal path is quiet, and you reach your destination along the level ground at the foot of the central hills with no difficulties.

To move north to the base of the island's highest peak, turn to **85**. To go south, turn to **100**.

27

Your journey across the island's northerly region is long, but straightforward and without challenge.

To progress north to the headland, turn to **50**. To continue south to the farm, turn to **141**.

28

Behind you, a thunderous crash precedes a plume of thick grey dust and dirt as the entire ground floor above the cellar collapses in. You leap up the nearby set of stairs as the choking cloud of crushed masonry and shattered bricks follow you upwards, threatening to consume you in its dark, suffocating embrace.

You are swift enough to avoid the worst effects of the dust, but you still arrive at the top of the stairs coughing uncontrollably after breathing the finer particles.

A dark corridor greets you with shards of sunlight beaming through the holes in a wooden door several feet ahead. You open it with a firm strike of your shoulder, and step into a study, half-filled with rubble from part of the collapsed ceiling.

Most of the furniture lies broken and covered by debris, and several dozen books lay ruined following years of exposure to the elements. A modest corner desk abutting the two remaining upright walls is the only intact furniture in this room. The desk's wood is old and rotten, and you break open the drawer with ease. Within, it presents you with several documents: Letters, a diary, and most interesting of all, a hand-drawn map.

It shows a coastal path with a small island drawn near to the larger landmass. The island is then drawn from a side view, with a point of interest between two outcrops. Finally, inscribed on the paper is an unusually shaped and marked mass. A boulder or a small stone? You have no sense of scale for this object.

Add the codeword **OUTER**.

Add **Phorbantia Treasure Map** to your inventory. Note this section number alongside it as you may wish to refer to the image in future.

The letters and diary are dated several centuries ago and are remarkably well preserved, protected by a simple metal case. They detail the struggles of Galene, an Imperial councillor, and her attempts to evacuate the island after violent fluctuations from the Divine Fire started to affect the land. The Office of the High Consul, ignoring her pleas, was more interested in the progress of the monument to the four pillars of the Empire being erected in the island's east.

The last entry in the diary reads.

> *8 Aprilis IA25. The Fire has strengthened for the fifth day and shows no sign of abating. Along with it, the black fog has also returned and we again exist in a permanent night. I am writing this as the last of my candles burns to the wick. The scratches and chattering at the door now drive me to consider the unthinkable.*
>
> *This darkness has never lasted longer than five days before. I guess tomorrow I will discover if I am in the gods' favour.*

Turn to **124** and mark the villa as complete.

29

Add the codeword **CABAL**.

You now hold all four keys to open the tomb of Niketas Aurelius. You just now need to locate it.

Return to the section number you were previously on and continue reading.

30

If you rolled no dice and failed the previous test on purpose, add 1 point to the ⬙ symbol (W) on your character sheet.

The leader steps back and looks at you, deeply contemplating your efforts through each of the trials, and ultimately, your fate.

If you passed 0 or 1 test, turn to **126**.

If you passed 2 or 3 tests, turn to **180**.

31

There is nothing else of interest on this stretch of path, and you continue your way.

To turn west towards the sea, turn to **118**. To proceed east to a T junction, turn to **68**.

32

This area's trails are the most treacherous you have so far encountered. The rocks are cracked and covered with thick moss and shrubs, and the angles of these stones as they slope downwards towards the sea mean you could slip and fall at any moment.

However, the rocks are jagged and rough, which allows purchase even along the steeper parts, and you can traverse them at a reduced pace with some confidence.

If you have already marked the box below against the current chapter, turn to **9**.

Otherwise, mark the box below against the current chapter and turn to that section number.

Chapter I, turn to **74**. ☐

Chapter II, turn to **187**. ☐

Chapter III, turn to **121**. ☐

33

The cave is deceptively deep yet retains a pleasant warmth from the morning sun, while also offering protection from the brisk wind battering the coast. You lay your clothing out on the rocks in the sun and settle down on a patch of thick grey moss to rest. Your ordeals of the day have depleted your energy and you soon drift off into a dreamless slumber.

Waking a few hours later, you feel refreshed and invigorated by the rest. Your clothes are dry, which leaves you in good spirits as you dress, and you head inland with determination in your step.

Add 1 marker to the time track.

Add 2 points to your Health.

Then you head eastwards. Turn to **164**.

34

Add 1 marker to the time track.

The trees open into lush green grassland with several buildings arranged in the centre. You approach and see several empty and partially collapsed buildings surrounding a small, cobbled square. Large piles of rubble mark the spots where structures once stood but have now extensively collapsed.

At the centre of the square is a smooth, bowl-shaped feature carved from a single block of stone. The crumbling remains of ornate shapes and figures lie submerged within. Dry green stains point to its function as a fountain or other similar decorative feature, and a couple of inches of muddy brown water sit at the bottom.

Dozens of inch-wide circular holes are carved into the bowl, accounting for the lack of liquid within.

Turn to **124**.

35

The wind and rain combine to create the absolute worst conditions for negotiating this flank of the mountain, and the steep slope offers countless surprises and dangers for the inexperienced climber. Hand and footholds collapse with the slightest movement, and you cannot use any of these with confidence to bear your weight.

You must rely on awkward crevasses and protrusions to pull yourself along, relying on your brute strength alone to cover the distance. Your arms and legs burn with the constant effort.

Make a check against your Physical ability. Add a +2 modifier if you have the Climbing skill.

If you gain 1 or more successes, turn to **125**. If not, turn to **163**.

Chapter II

The calm, sunny, and pleasant warm weather you have enjoyed on the island since your arrival abruptly changes. From the east coast, an angry black cloud rolls over the entire area. The heavens open to a torrent of rain. Lightning and thunder accompany the deluge, which soon soaks your clothes through. Clouds race to the west, and fleeting moments of sunny calm are swiftly replaced with more storms.

Remove any effects that expire at the end of a chapter. If you were instructed to add more markers to the time track than were available in Chapter I, add these additional ones at the start of Chapter II.

Return to the section you were previously on and continue reading.

37

You skilfully negotiate this stretch of trail without incident.

To go southeast to the coast, turn to **190**. To move northwest into the thick jungle, turn to **82**.

38

The sea rolls and undulates with angry violence, peppering you with spray at each peak of the waves crashing against the rocks.

Distracted by the clamour and undulating power of the sea, a large trough forms unnoticed by you in the swell, followed immediately after by a wall of white, foaming seawater. The wave knocks you off your feet where the retreating surge then sweeps you helplessly out to sea.

Your survival instinct kicks in, and you swim frantically back to shore, the conditions and your waterlogged clothes making it a punishing return. You are bleeding profusely from a deep gash you suffered being dragged by the sea over the sharp rocks.

Lose 3 Health.

Add 1 marker to the time track as you recover from your ordeal.

To continue east, turn to **17**. To travel west, turn to **143**.

39

You edge towards the boat. Carefully using crates, barrels, and rubble, you also gain the benefit of some lucky timing to avoid the gaze of the unaware pirates. They continue about their business, oblivious to you or anyone else on the island, as you crawl and slip between cover.

Make a check against your Agility ability. Add a +1 modifier if you have the Sneak skill.

If you gain at least 1 success and have the codeword **FEAST**, turn to **147**.

If you gain at least 1 success and do not have the codeword **FEAST**, turn to **53**.

If you fail to gain at least 1 success, turn to **132**.

40

"That is a shame." the man sounds a shade offended, but is polite, and mentions nothing further on the subject. Your two hosts both quaff from their goblets, and the conversation is jolly, if now somewhat slurred at points.

The lady lights one of the incense sticks protruding from a clay jar and breathes deeply of the aroma. The sweet lavender fragrance is pleasant and floral.

You chat at length about how the couple survives in such a remote location living off the land, and the old man, several goblets of wine loosening his tongue, offers a cursory explanation. He leans in, as if hiding the conversation from a non-existent eavesdropper, and whispers.

"Hunting and foraging are easy if you have the right skills and equipment. Finding an abandoned cellar full of wine uses a bit more luck." he laughs and raises his goblet. You laugh with him at the forthright admission and raise an invisible glass to toast good fortune.

Turn to **182**.

41

You place the four hexagonal keys into the slots and a low rumbling is followed by the rock wall sliding downwards, revealing a narrow chamber on the other side.

A glowing yellow glass sphere, set atop an unassuming circular altar, illuminates the chamber in a warm glow. Frescoes and text of the pantheons of gods, both Roman and Greek, from early Republic times adorn the white plaster walls. Aged over a thousand years old, they are overdrawn, in part, by images of the Divine Fire from centuries later.

Along the wall on your left, a raised stone slab, a few inches above floor height and almost 7 feet long, marks the location of General Aurelius' tomb. It is a modest affair and only records the following text.

NIKETAS.AVRELIVS.IA.CCXV

Behind the altar is a suit of golden armour in the classical legionary style. It is feather-light, and the tough, seemingly unbreakable metal remains untarnished by the years.

If you take the armour, add the codeword **VAGUE**.

Add **Golden Legionary Armour [Light Armour +6]** to your inventory.

You must now return east. Turn to **188**.

42

Add 2 markers to the time track.

You clamber aboard the raft after your ordeal with the shark and, lying flat on your front, you kick and paddle with relative ease. You are not as animated in your strokes as your approach to the raft, but your journey nevertheless progresses swiftly to the island.

The navy is too busy roughly fishing survivors from the water to chase after a lone escapee now. You know that the penalty for approaching closer than ten leagues to Sicilia is death, and you are also well aware of the brutal interrogations the survivors can expect to receive before that end.

You lock those thoughts far from your mind as you could not help anyone without perishing yourself. After several hours, the waters become lighter in hue, and in no time you see the rocky seabed below. Ahead of you is a beach and you clamber off the raft and wade to shore.

Turn to **98**.

43

The eastern side of this windswept northerly trail is bordered by a lush green wood, impassable with dense, thick foliage. To the west, a flat plain of verdant grass drops towards the rocky cliffs overlooking the blue rolling sea. To the north, the path passes through fertile farmland and to the south, the treeline extends as the island widens.

If you have already marked the box below against the current chapter, turn to **178**.

Otherwise, mark the box below against the current chapter and turn to that section number.

Chapter I, turn to **89**. ☐

Chapter II, turn to **113**. ☐

Chapter III, turn to **20**. ☐

44

You strip to your shirt and trousers and swim for your life towards the nearby land. Leaving behind all your worldly possessions, they sink to the bottom of the Mediterranean, joining the transport that you were, until recently, enjoying a peaceful sleep upon.

Remove **Dagger [Small Melee +0]** and **Leather Brigandine [Light Armour +1]** from your inventory.

The weather is calm, but the waves remain animated and rough in contrast. The constant undulations of the sea sap your strength and morale, and your efforts, while beginning with much energy and enthusiasm, now lack progress.

To make your situation more difficult, the blood in the water, combined with your splashing, attracts the attention of this stretch of water's less pleasant of residents.

The terrifying sight of triple dorsal fins heading your way from the left gives you mere moments to prepare for the impact. The creature, a fan shark you surmise from the flickering of the fins, is only 3 feet long but is extremely quick and, from its aggression, intensely hungry.

Make a check against your Physical ability. Add a +1 modifier if you have the Swimming skill.

If you gain at least 1 success, turn to **162**. If not, turn to **86**.

45

The last animated host collapses to the ground. The sap that gave life to these creatures turns a milky grey, and its power, now extinguished, causes the wounds and lesions to relax and widen. Their husks burst open into stinking piles of bloated, rotten flesh.

You approach the tree and observe the deep purple sap that drips to the ground now flows towards the corpses. Pulling the bark easily apart from a slit down the length of the tree, you are horrified to see a fleshy organ pumping the sap via thick red arteries where the solid trunk of the tree should be.

You sense movement behind you as the nearest corpse to the tree stands up. The heart is muscular yet vulnerable as any meat. It appears you could destroy it with little effort.

The powerful flow of sap from the pumping heart forms ripples in the wood, and you recognise from experience this kill will not be clean. The tree's 'blood' will certainly spray some distance, maybe even hitting you if you are close enough.

If you wish to destroy the heart, turn to **84**. To leave the clearing, turn to **12**.

46

The path that connects the summit of the highest peak on the isle and the western coast meanders lazily from base to peak. It makes for a much easier traversal considering the height difference.

If you have already marked the box below against the current chapter, turn to **120**.

Otherwise, mark the box below against the current chapter and turn to that section number.

Chapter I, turn to **77**. ☐

Chapter II, turn to **158**. ☐

Chapter III, turn to **2**. ☐

47

You strip to your undergarments and wade out into the bay. With momentary hesitation, you let yourself sink below the surface, and you gasp and gag as the saltwater fills your lungs. The power of water breathing takes immediate effect, and each drawn breath feels unnatural and uncomfortable. It takes a few minutes to adjust to this environment, but you are soon breathing as normal.

Any companion remains on the shore and cannot assist you while you are in the wreck.

You dive to the hull of the ship through light blue waters, crystal clear for a remarkable distance, and enter through a gaping hole in its side. The hull is teeming with aquatic life, beautifully coloured fish dart through the water and others feed upon the algae that covers the wood.

Pushing forward, the deck rises over the rocks, impaling the ship. Soon, you are standing on a dark transport deck, waist deep in water, breathing air once again.

Seeing there are many crates in this section, you approach one to investigate the contents.

Pulling a rotten wooden lid from one, three black snakelike creatures lunge from the newly created hole at you.

Their bodies are thick, broader than your thigh, and their jaws contain rows of sharp teeth, formed with perfection to rip flesh from bone.

You must fight.

	Weapons	Health	
Mutant Moray Eel	1	2	
Mutant Moray Eel	1	2	
Mutant Moray Eel	1	2	

You cannot escape as the eels are much faster swimmers than you and will tear you apart before you can reach safety.

If you win, turn to **165**.

48

You charge into the clearing and are straight away set upon by one beetle. The other concentrates its attacks on the alta.

During this combat, if one combatant kills their opponent, they will assist their ally in the other fight.

The peregrine alta is an ally in this combat, and you will control his attacks on the beetles. He has **8 Clear [Air] Crystals** and will use these in combat if instructed.

He is equipped with a **Spear [Small Melee +2]** and **Scalemail [Light Armour +3]**.

When he reaches a Health of 3 or below, he will use a crystal to heal himself. He will only use a crystal to heal your character in combat should you reach a Health of 3 or below and you have no other healing available.

	Weapons	Health	
Giant Beetle	3	2	
Giant Beetle	3	3	

	Weapons	Mystical	Armour	Health	
Peregrine Alta	2	2	3	8	

The beetles are quick, but they have ample food nearby and will not attempt to catch an insignificant and elusive prey. To escape, add 1 point to the 🛡 symbol (G) on your character sheet, and turn to **176**.

If you win and the alta survives, turn to **130**. If you win and he dies, turn to **87**.

49

As you pass under the sheerest portion of the mountain, an overhang many hundreds of feet above creates a sense of vulnerability with the enormity of the geology on the small island.

You quicken your pace to avoid the almost inevitable crushing rockfall. The aeons of erosion do not trigger the deadly landslide you fear, but you are nonetheless relieved after safely passing by.

Your heart jumps as a shadow emerges on the rocky ground ahead and then disappears from the edge of your vision. Loud screeching fills the air as if several gulls were targeting food, and you jolt your head back to see what caused the shadow.

Nothing now is visible, but the loud screeches continue in the distance, obscured by the low clouds and mountains.

The calls then vanish as dramatically as they appeared. You continue onwards.

To travel north, turn to **85**. To proceed south, turn to **100**.

50

Add 1 marker to the time track.

You reach the northernmost tip of the island, the base of a headland that reaches high above the crashing waves of the Mediterranean.

To the east, on the island of Sicilia, a pillar of black smoke tinted with purple flashes rises high into the atmosphere where it dissipates flatly over the landscape.

North and west in the far distance, vessels sail on their business, avoiding the blockade. Imperial naval ships patrol these waters sporadically with orders to sink any boats and kill or capture any person foolish enough to approach the devastated lands.

Scattered ruins are the only curious points of interest in this area, and a half-collapsed grain store in a small hollow near the water's edge offers the closest opportunity. Investigating the store, you find piles of damp firewood, and this gives you an idea.

You could, with the right equipment and abilities, create a fire with the wood which may attract the attention of a passing ship. If they investigated, you might then gain passage away from the island.

The firewood is damp from exposure to the elements. You need an accelerant, and means to ignite it, for this plan to succeed.

The store has several lengths of rope securing the firewood, and you can take one if you wish. Add **20ft of Rope [Equipment]** to your inventory if you do so.

If you wish to leave the island, you must have a **Bottle of Oil** in your inventory and one of the following means to create fire:
  - **Flint** or **Flint and Steel** in your inventory, or
  - A Mystical ability of at least level 1, and **1 Red Crystal [Fire]** (remove if used), or
  - One Prayer available (remove if used), and a patron god's keyword of [Fire], or
  - Other means with which you can cause 1 point of damage with a keyword of [Fire].

If you have the means and want to leave the island, turn to **78**.

Otherwise, your only option is to return south. Turn to **177**.

51

Add 1 marker to the time track.

Even after your ordeals of the past few minutes, you make excellent progress to the island. With no heavy equipment encumbering your advance, the waters eventually become lighter in hue. Finally, you can stand on the rocky seafloor and wade to shore.

Turn to **98**.

52

Your trek along the dim and shadowy coast is uneventful. Several stretches show evidence of the storm that struck the island not long ago, and the results of several violent wave impacts are evident on the trail after striking the pathway and surging inland.

To move east, turn to **17**. To journey west, turn to **143**.

53

You deftly sneak towards the boat, unseen by any of the pirates on that final stretch. As you crouch, preparing to cross the last few feet to the vessel, a boy, barely a dozen years behind him, steps from the boat onto the jetty ahead of you and turns to drop a handful of olive seeds into the water.

Your eyes meet and you hold your trembling breath as he looks you up and down. He seems to sway on his feet and his eyes are unfocused as he squints at you, trying to remember if he has met you before. A silver goblet lies on its side on top of a barrel on deck, his apparent cause for confusion. He shrugs and holds out his hand palm upwards towards you.

"You want this boat, don't you?" His slurred question is rhetorical, yet you nod an affirmative at him. He pauses for a moment to consider his options.

"60 coins if you want passage," he demands.

He is too far away to take down quietly, and you would not get 5 feet before he alerted the entire camp to your presence.

If you have 60 denarii on your person and wish to pay, turn to **16**.

If you are unable or unwilling to pay this amount, turn to **102**.

54

Due to your previous experience along this path, you traverse even the most troublesome parts of this treacherous route with no problems.

To progress east, turn to **190**. To head west, turn to **88**.

55

You descend the gentle slope of the hill that heads down into the calm bay. Many dozens of bottles float in the water from the destroyed crates, and a couple have broken against the shore, imparting rocks and water alike with a slick black shine.

Add a **Bottle of Oil [Consumable]** to your inventory if you do not carry one.

There is nothing else of interest in this area, so you exit northwest. Turn to **190**.

56

The villa's facade seemed untouched by the ravages that impacted other buildings in the village, however you notice as you enter the central courtyard, the rest of the building has not fared as well. The red-tiled roof has collapsed onto the upper floor at the rear, and the entire back section of the ground floor is rubble. To your left is a broken window, your only means of entry.

You climb through into a dank and dusty antechamber with an ornate wooden door, slightly ajar, leading into a further room. You approach the door and without warning, the ancient rotten floorboards collapse under your weight, sending you tumbling into the darkness below.

Lose 1 Health from the sudden fall and awkward landing.

Turn to **169**.

57

Add the codeword **MINOR**.

To one side of the path, its clothes and bones bleached white as chalk, lies the skeleton of a long-deceased traveller. Tattered clothing hangs off the bones, and it clasps a heavy leather pouch with broken fingers, tight to the body. One of the poor explorer's legs is broken above the knee, and you can only surmise how and when this happened before they perished.

You open the pouch and find a purse containing some red crystals, a few sticks of charcoal, and a map of an island called 'Phorbantia' with some cryptic notes and strange symbols.

There is also a quiver of arrows several feet from the body, and alongside those, a shortbow.

Add **10 Red Crystals [Fire]** and **Shortbow [Large Ranged +1]** to your inventory.

Turn to **200**.

58

As you had savagely experienced before, your mere presence seems to usher forth powerful bolts of bright blue lightning emitting from the forest floor. Powerful lances of energy shoot to the sky, striking the canopy with frightening power, leaving scorch marks and holes on the black, smoking leaves.

You cautiously approach following your previous encounter here, yet the lightning has increased in magnitude and is at such strength that you cannot proceed without severe risk to your life.

You cannot continue and must turn back the way you came. To the west are the ruins of a village, and eastwards, you spy the apex of a ruined temple rising above the trees.

If you want to return west to the village, turn to **34**. To retreat east to the temple, turn to **82**.

59

You stand at a crossroads. To the west, the path hugs the north face of the island's highest peak. The steep rocky faces are impassable, but to the southwest is a narrow path that winds its way up a gentler incline towards the summit, several hundred feet above the sea.

To the southeast, the path is level and flanked either side by heavily forested tracts. Northeast, the trail gradually descends and skirts around the northern edge of the woodland.

If you wish to head west around the base of the mountain, turn to **7**. To proceed southwest and climb the mountain, turn to **90**. If you want to go southeast, turn to **167**. To travel northeast, turn to **146**.

60

"Hmm," the pirate leader scratches his ear but remains emotionless after your story. He continues after a few moments pause. "Right. Let's see how good you are with your fists."

A tall, burly, and stern man steps forward. Well over six and a half feet tall, broad-shouldered, and thick-limbed, he has hands that could crush stone and his scarred face has visibly seen more than its fair share of violence.

You must fight this bruiser bare-handed using your Weapons ability. You will fight him alone. Remember, if you do not have the Brawling skill, you require a 5+ to hit.

The crowd will closely watch this contest. You may not use any other help, such as spells, items, powers, or prayers in this combat. Any companion remains safely hidden out of sight.

If you do, you forfeit the fight, which ends then as you get set upon by the angry spectators.

Do not reduce your Health with any damage taken as this fist fight does not cause permanent damage. As soon as he reduces you to zero Health, you are knocked out rather than killed and the fight is lost.

	Weapons	Health	
Pirate Bruiser	3	4	☐

If you win, note you have passed this test.

If he knocks you out, or you forfeit the fight, reduce your Health by 2 points as the severe beating you receive caused some painful internal damage.

Turn to **142**.

61

The border of the lush jungle covering a large area of the eastern part of the island is a thick, imposing wall of deep green foliage that is, in most places, impassable. It contrasts starkly with the pale brown dirt, sandstone rocks, and muted greens of the brush and grass in the west.

The single trail you walk at present provides the only means of possible travel.

If you have already marked the box below against the current chapter, turn to **37**.

Otherwise, mark the box below against the current chapter and turn to that section number.

Chapter I, turn to **8**.   ☐

Chapter II, turn to **153**.   ☐

Chapter III, turn to **122**.   ☐

62

The storms that hitherto lashed the area have since retreated, leaving loose rocks and sodden dirt on the mountainside trail. At this height, the gloom of the thick black mist considerably impairs your vision and judgement, making difficult progress even harsher. The path is little more than a narrow rocky ledge in places and your body burns with the sustained effort and exertion.

Make a check against your Agility ability. Add a +2 modifier if you have the Climbing skill.

Then, make a check against your Physical ability. Add a +2 modifier if you have the Strength skill.

If you pass both tests, turn to **125**. If you fail at least one test, turn to **23**.

63

The air is warm in the late morning sun, but the brisk sea wind drives inland with force and you shiver uncontrollably from the chill. Heading east, you soon falter, suffering from the effects of exposure as you climb the winding rocky path leading further inland.

Lose 1 point of Health as your body fights the effects of the elements.

Turn to **164**.

64

The open road and light grey cobblestones provide a small amount of guidance in the darkness, and you make good progress along its length. To one side, where the easternmost trees grow even further back from the trail, a dark patch in the pale grass causes you to pause for one moment.

Upon a closer investigation, you observe the dark patch is actually a large sink hole, thirty feet or more in diameter, that has recently opened. Rocks, stones, and lumps of dirt from the edges drop intermittently into its depths, and you peer into the opening. The darkness that envelops the isle obscures your view and you cannot clearly see how deep the void reaches.

A sole tree stands defiantly next to the pit with roots protruding into the blackness. You decide against using any powers to explore as a way out may not be available after their use.

If you have **Rope** in your inventory with a length of at least 20ft, and you wish to descend, turn to **22**.

Otherwise, to resume north, turn to **34**. To journey south, turn to **88**.

65

The pirates scramble to grab their weapons as the sudden combat ensues. You are soon surrounded and blows rain down upon you from the chaotic melee. Your companion, if you have one, upon observing your struggles, rushes at once into the fray to assist.

Only four pirates can attack you at one time, and you can only attack these four in melee combat. When one dies, the next on the list without an opponent takes their place.

As you have the element of surprise, you plus any companions and allies have one free combat round at the start of the fight, with no enemy attacks in that first round. Once this round is resolved, begin a standard combat round as normal.

	Weapons	Health		
Quartermaster	2	3	☐	
Pirate 1	1	2	☐	
Pirate 2	2	1	☐	
Captain	4	3	☐	
First Mate	2	2	☐	
Pirate 3	1	2	☐	
Pirate 4	1	2	☐	
Bruiser	3	4	☐	
Navigator	2	2	☐	
Boatswain	2	2	☐	
Helmsman	1	3	☐	Crossbow [Large Ranged +0]
Master at Arms	2	2	☐	Flintlock Pistol [Small Ranged +0]

With the vast number of pirates confronting you, there is no chance of escape from this arguably brave and, as an observer might declare, foolhardy encounter.

When the captain and at least five other pirates are dead, turn to **106**.

66

The spectral wolves instinctively look up as you approach and snarl with an unnatural and guttural hiss. The largest of the three aims a couple of vicious barks towards you and arches its back, hackles bristling, in an intimidating display of confidence and strength.

You advance with caution as the wolves gauge their new opponent. The standoff lasts just a few seconds until, with teeth bared and a flash of yellow in their eyes, they leap towards you in unison at a shocking preternatural pace.

Their lack of physical form does nothing to temper the wounds these beasts cause. You are thankful this means they can suffer damage from you.

Any damage with a keyword of [Air] is doubled against the wolves.

	Weapons	Health	
Spectral Wolf	1	3	☐
Spectral Wolf	1	3	☐
Spectral Wolf	1	2	☐

If you wish to flee the combat, the wolves will not give chase. Add 1 point to the symbol (G) on your character sheet. To retreat towards the northernmost headland, turn to **177**. If you wish to flee south, deeper into the island, turn to **43**.

If you win, turn to **136**.

67

You ascend to the nest on the mountaintop and find it devoid of life. The egg, however, has hatched and now lies in pieces on the nest's floor. Its previous occupant long since departed.

To descend the mountain and journey east, turn to **90**. To descend and head west, turn to **46**.

68

You are now at a T junction with two other routes branching from the track along which you arrived. To the north, the land flattens out and you see farmland in the distance. Westward, a narrow winding path leads down towards a sheltered cove and the sea. To the south, the ground ascends further inland, where the lofty peaks on its westerly flank jut from the thick forest canopy.

To advance north towards the farm, turn to **43**. If you wish to proceed west down towards the cove, turn to **164**. To move south deeper into the island, turn to **146**.

69

You have returned to the islet where you discovered the hidden chest. This has since washed into the seas by the powerful, crashing waves. Nothing else of interest remains for you on this part of the island.

You must retrace your steps and resume your journey northeast. Turn to **143**.

70

Add the codewords **BENCH** and **QUILL**.

Regulus is dead. You may take his **Spear [Small Melee +2]** and any unused crystals in his inventory.

His remaining equipment is not useful or valuable to you, but he does have a note and a simple metal ring in one pocket.

You read the note, a love letter of quite incredible emotion and thought. Within, you discover he was to marry someone named Sabina in the city of Aquileia, north of Roma in the province of Italia. You should take the information of his demise to his lover.

Add **Note from Regulus and Ring** to your inventory.

Add **Entry 2 - Return the wedding ring (Aquileia - I)** to your journal

Return to the volume and section you were previously on and continue reading.

71

You approach the obelisk once again. The hum that greeted you on your first encounter is silent and its previous energy dissipated. There is nothing further of interest in the area, but you can gather flint if needed.

Add **Flint** to your inventory.

If you wish to head north, turn to **150**. If you wish to go south, turn to **32**.

72

Book of Legends: The Eternal Empire

Volume 0 - Prologue

Chapter III

As abruptly as the storm had started, the rain, thunder, and lightning vanish from the skies. The clouds, however, remain and settle lower over the island, enveloping it in a dark grey haze. It is tinged with an acrid, burning odour and makes breathing with light exertion, or even walking, painful and laboured.

The sun is now but a muted, glowing patch of luminescence in the dark smoke, casting light as a full moon might on a thick, cloudy night.

The air is almost silent. Not a period of calm peace, but subdued, with sounds of the sea and wildlife muted. It is impossible to pinpoint the direction or distance of anything audible and only sounds nearby are discernible with any accuracy.

Remove any effects that expire at the end of a chapter. If you were instructed to add more markers to the time track than were available in Chapter II, add any additional markers at the start of Chapter III.

Your regular income and expenses now become due. Add or remove your income and expenses total from the Imperial Treasury balance on your character sheet.

If you cannot afford to pay any expenses from the treasury, deduct the rest from the amount you hold on your person. If you are unable or unwilling to make up the shortfall, you must remove that item or benefit from your character sheet at once.

Return to the section you were previously on and continue reading.

73

You open the door and enter a spacious wine cellar. Ancient bottles sit in racks, covered in dust and cobwebs. Wooden boxes, packed with hay and containing more bottles, are placed against the walls. Two square areas of the floor, matching a crate's footprint, are clear of dust and it is evident two were moved in the recent past.

You spy through the low light a small chest in one corner. Opening it, you find a small amount of money and a couple of vivid purple crystals.

Add **10 Denarii** and **2 Purple Crystals [Aether]** to your inventory.

The sound of falling masonry becomes steadily louder, interrupting your search. You rush from the room as the collapse begins.

Make a check against your Agility ability. Add a +1 modifier if you have the Athletics skill.

If you fail to gain at least 1 success, remove 2 points from your Health as a heavy brick strikes you with force to the head. If you gain 1 or more successes, you escape this injury by mere inches.

You clamber towards the stairs. Turn to **28**.

74

The rocks underfoot close to the sea are grey and lifeless, contrasting against the cliffs set further back, which are bright with colour. The deep brown and orange-hued stones complement the pigments of the dry grasses and plant life, that flourish away from the shore.

Impressive and vivid scenery aside, your journey through this area otherwise passes without incident.

To continue north, turn to **100**. To continue south, turn to **143**.

75

The barn is cavernous, and the floor is strewn with the fossilised remains of straw, seeds, and hempen sacks. A skeleton lies prone on the ground, clutching a short sword in the bony remains of its right hand. The ill-fated figure's head has been crushed by some unknown force, and the skull lies shattered in pieces.

The sword is of good quality and shows no signs of rust or other wear.

Add **Short Sword [Small Melee +1]** to your inventory.

There is nothing else of interest or value in the barn.

Turn to **124** and mark the checkbox next to the Barn as complete.

76

You are fully submerged in the dark blue Mediterranean waters, and you must fight hard to stop yourself from being pulled further into the deep by the sinking ship.

You kick hard as your head breaks the water and you suck in the much-needed air. Something brushes past your leg and you flinch instinctively. It could be a shark you witnessed earlier, and that is a massive concern. This close to Sicilia, however, means it might be something *much* worse.

You must decide now what your next course of action will be.

Land is but a mile away. A rugged island disconnected from the main Sicilian landmass, and which must be your target now. It looks extensive enough for you to avoid any pursuers there should they be intent on following.

A sizeable barrel bobs in the water nearby. Larger than your own body, it would allow you to cling to one side and hide from the navy as they pick up survivors.

Towards the island, a large raft of wood, blown from the ship's hull, floats a few hundred yards away. This could prove a quicker escape than clinging to the barrel, but you are unsure you can cover the distance in your armour.

Finally, you could swim directly to the island, reaching it within just an hour or two. You would need to strip to your lightest clothes and drop all equipment to achieve that.

If you want to cling to the barrel, turn to **152**.

To swim towards the raft, turn to **131**.

To head directly to the island, turn to **44**.

77

The trail is curiously well trodden for such a remote and difficult part of the island, and some footprints baked in the dry mud are distinctly non-human.

Two enormous boulders ahead create a narrow passage into which the path continues. Proceeding forward, the forms of four small humanoids, a drab, flaxen-yellow hue to their thick wrinkly skin, emerge from between the boulders.

They carry an assortment of crude serrated blades, tarnished with age yet glinting at the edges from regular sharpening. Leather slings hang from string belts and their rough leather armour is cobbled together in a patchwork from a variety of cured skins.

They do not spot you as they negotiate the rock passage, but afterwards identify you as a hostile right away. You recognise the form of a Sinapis Ferocis, a small and aggressive gremlin-like creature whose wild temperament and territorial behaviour almost always results in combat when encountering them.

They utter guttural, unintelligible, grunts and snorts from their throats and move in a line towards you. On the narrow path, only you or one companion/ally can fight one enemy in melee combat, replacing any dead opponent with the next in the list.

The creatures are each armed with a Rusty Blade [Small Melee +1] and a Sling [Small Ranged +0]. Any opponent who is not in melee combat will attack using their sling.

	Weapons	Health	
Sinapis Ferocis	2	1	☐
Sinapis Ferocis	2	1	☐
Sinapis Ferocis	2	1	☐
Sinapis Ferocis	2	1	☐

You can escape at any time. If so, take one ranged attack from each remaining enemy as you flee and add 1 point to the  symbol (G) on your character sheet. You must return in the same direction from which you arrived at this encounter.

To retreat west towards the coast, turn to **85**. To return east up the mountain, turn to **133**.

If you win, turn to **128**.

78

Remove **Bottle of Oil** from your inventory

You wait until the seas are clear of any naval ships that might cause trouble and pour the oil liberally over the piles of wood. The thick, sticky black liquid oozes between the timbers, and you light the base. The oil briskly does its task and the flames comfortably take hold, sizzling and crackling on the damp wood.

Thick grey smoke reaches high from the headland and is carried north by the wind. A speck in the distance becomes larger and soon you can make out a small trading cog on its approach. The ocean is otherwise clear of ships and you can clamber down the low, stepped cliff to set foot on a thin strip of rocky shore.

"Hail, stranger" The captain shouts, a young woman with angular features and salt-washed hair. She looks at you up and down to take a measure of your worth, and happy with your ability to work off your passage on her ship, continues.

"Quickly now, the navy patrols like hungry sharks here."

You step aboard the ship and with haste, depart from the island. Once you are finally in open water and free from danger, you relax. Having escaped the island, you will now continue to the next stage of your adventure.

Remove **Entry 1 - Escape from Phorbantia** from your journal if it is active.

Add 5 ability points and spend them on improving any secondary abilities if you wish. Gaining levels in primary abilities requires specialist training and you may not improve these right now. You may save any unused points for later.

Add the codeword **INGOT**.

Increase your Health and Prayers to their maximum values, and remove any effects that expire when you leave a volume. Any companion will now depart your service.

Turn to Section **127** in Volume I.

79

Although the rain has ceased and the ground has begun drying out in patches over this area, the path is still treacherous with wet rocks and dirt loosened by the deluge. The Sicilian smoke sorely tests your judgement of each step in the darkness, but you stumble onwards regardless.

Make a check against your Agility ability. Add a +1 modifier if you have the Reflexes skill.

If you gain at least 1 success, turn to **137**. If not, turn to **4**.

80

The shark keeps its teeth embedded firmly in your leg and you feebly kick to dislodge its hold on you. You struggle hard, yet your strength is no match against your determined attacker.

However, your luck might well be. A sailor is dragged at speed past you, gurgling and screaming a horrifying wail before being silenced as he is pulled beneath the waves. The sea is red with his blood and entrails, and your attacker, sensing the feed spreading around it, enters a frenzy.

It lets your leg go for just a single moment. Now free from its jaws, you kick hard through the blood filled water towards the raft on your escape. Powering forward in panic, all elegance and wariness long since departed, you race for your life from those creatures, man and beast, that wish you ill in this small corner of the sea.

The screams of death abate in a short matter of time, one small consolation for the unfortunate victims.

Lose 3 Health.

Turn to **42**.

81

The door to the temple you had opened before is closed since your last visit, but using the hexagonal keys, you reopen the tomb. The room remains empty and you return east. Turn to **188**.

82

Add 1 marker to the time track.

If you have the codewords **BENCH** and **REMIT**, turn to **154**.

If you have the codeword **BENCH** (but not **REMIT**), turn to **199**.

If you have the codeword **REMIT** (but not **BENCH**), turn to **105**.

Otherwise, turn to **14**.

83

You return to the farm where you fought the spectral wolves harassing the farmers. The couple are now sitting outside enjoying their newfound peace and they are delighted to see you again.

"Friend!" the woman exclaims. "Please, if you need to rest, our door is always open to you."

She beckons towards the farmhouse and you may accept the kind offer of a warm and safe bed.

No matter if you rest or not, afterwards there are no reasons to remain and you must depart.

To go towards the northernmost headland, turn to **177**. To travel south, deeper into the island, turn to **43**.

84

The heart will die by one hit from a weapon or spell, or a few seconds of pulling and tearing if you are unarmed, but you may choose any method to cause 1 point of damage.

Upon being wounded, the sap splashing from the wounds reeks harshly of sulphur and the burst is so powerful that droplets burn the ground from the spatter several feet away.

Lose 2 points of Health from the splashes of the sap if you used a melee attack with a weapon, or lose 4 Health if you are unarmed. This is a combat attack and you will reduce damage with rolls against your armour rating and defensive agility bonus as appropriate.

No damage is incurred from a ranged attack.

The heart is now destroyed. Promptly, the animated hosts collapse back to the ground, this time for evermore as they fall apart in a squelching mess on impact.

Add the codeword **NOVEL**.

Add 1 point to the  symbol (F) on your character sheet.

A further search of the area reveals nothing else of interest and you must now exit the clearing. If you wish to journey north, turn to **146**. If you would like to move south, turn to **198**.

85

You arrive at a T junction. To the east is a wide path that narrows as it winds up a mountainside to its peak. North is a short path that you see ends in another junction, while to the south the path meanders along the western coast of the island.

To head east up the mountain, turn to **46**. If you want to proceed north, turn to **188**. To journey south, turn to **150**.

86

The shark dives towards you with an astonishing speed and you are helpless to defend yourself. You are fortunate that it is a small creature, yet its jaws are still powerful, and it clamps them into your waist.

The dark seas of the Mediterranean cover your head as you drop beneath the waves, your frantic gasps allowing the salty water to enter your lungs. You are fighting for your life and your head breaches the surface again as you cough and gag for air.

Twisting in the water, you pound the shark's head hard until it lets go, retreating to hunt less challenging prey. You are then free to swim, bleeding and tired, once again towards the island.

Lose 3 points from your Health.

Turn to **51**.

Add the codewords **BENCH** and **QUILL**.

The fight is finally over, and the giant beetles are now dead. Apart from the ruined temple, a crumbling edifice to the four pillars of the Eternal Empire, there only remains you and the lifeless body of the alta.

You may take his **Spear [Small Melee +2]** and add it to your inventory.

He also has a note and a simple metal ring in his pocket. You read the note, a love letter of quite incredible emotion and thought, and discover he was to marry someone named Sabina in the city of Aquileia, north of Roma in the province of Italia. You should take the information of his demise to his lover.

Add **Note from Regulus and Ring** to your inventory.

Add **Entry 2 - Return the wedding ring (Aquileia - I)** to your journal

There is nothing else within the clearing save a few scraps of cloth, bone, and dark patches of blood on the floor. A fitting vignette of the land you explore.

If you wish to leave the clearing and continue west to the centre of the island, turn to **11**. To move southeast towards the eastern coast, turn to **61**.

88

You reach a T junction. To the north, a well built cobbled road enters a bright golden wood. Eastwards, it runs into the distance along the south coast of the island.

To the south, the road continues a short distance before dropping to the coast. You can just make out the tip of a ship's mast peeking above the clifftop.

If you wish to travel north, turn to **156**. If you want to go east, turn to **110**. To progress south, turn to **17**.

89

Acres of farmland near the southernmost edge by the treeline show signs of severe plant and crop damage. Leaves and half-eaten vegetables lie scattered on the broken earth, and holes in the soil point to several possible nests.

The damage appears not too extensive and the substantial farmland remains mostly intact. The area is quiet at present in the warm sun and you proceed at pace to your next destination.

To advance north to the farm, turn to **141**. To resume south to a T junction, turn to **68**.

90

The eastern flank of the tallest peak on this isle is a steep and punishing trail. Progress is tortuously slow as you navigate the mountain path, with each step a test of both your bravery and luck as loose dirt under your boots trickles down the side of the mountain.

If you have already marked the box below against the current chapter, turn to **144**.

Otherwise, mark the box below against the current chapter and turn to that section number.

Chapter I, turn to **170**.   ☐

Chapter II, turn to **35**.   ☐

Chapter III, turn to **62**.   ☐

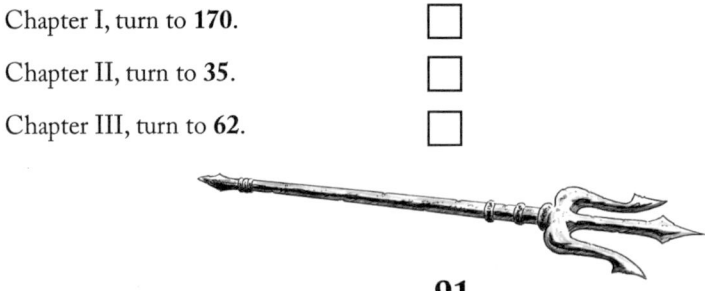

91

The dark black smoke that has enveloped the island clears with a brisk easterly wind. Through the last moments of its clearing, you are taken aback by the sight of a large Imperial Navy battleship a few hundred yards offshore and two rowboats of well armoured legionaries approaching the harbour.

Loud explosions are followed by screaming as a single broadside from the battleship scatters the pirates. Wood splinters and stone buildings explode with the might of the cannons. After some minutes, the salvoes cease as the legionaries disembark to finish the job.

You hide until the fighting concludes, just a few minutes later, and as the army finishes off the last of the settlement's occupants, you make yourself known. Several legionaries size you up briefly and advance at pace with violence in their eyes.

Chains on several prisoners, former slaves to a band of now dead pirates, make your story an easier one to concoct. You explain that these brigands captured you, yet you escaped with some of their equipment to live off the land until help arrives.

The decanus, a tall and broad Durum, and the ranking officer of this group, ponders your tall story. The other slaves do not recognise you as a pirate and your immediate executed is stayed. With no reason to continue the violence, he eventually waves you away and you are safe for now.

In those moments of fear, you failed to spot the black smoke had returned, covering the island once more in its oppressive black embrace. A strange coincidence that the attack occurred at the exact moment the clouds, smoke, and dust cleared, returning only when the navy had completed its objectives.

You keep your thoughts silent. Your possible knowledge now of the capability of the naval magi is best left unspoken.

Add no further markers to the time track from this point in the volume. You may take unlimited rests for the rest of the volume as you explore the island at your leisure.

Add the codeword **DEITY**.

Turn to **114**.

92

You pass around the base of the mountain range on its northernmost edge. From high in the peaks, a distant roar breaks the relative peace. Booming around the jagged landscape, it is unclear from which direction the echoing source ultimately is.

There are a few moments of quiet before a second roar, further away, allays your fears of any immediate encounter.

To move southwest to a T junction, turn to **188**. To continue southeast to a crossroads, turn to **59**.

93

Your journey along the southerly coastal path is uneventful.

To continue east, turn to **17**. To head west, turn to **143**.

94

In the passing time since your arrival on this island, wreckage, fresh from a recent battle, is washed up on the shore. Crates, barrels, and shattered wood litter the rocky beach and cover the surface of the water in the small cove.

Searching the wreckage yields little in the way of interesting items, but some fresh fruit and cured meat provide a little subsistence. Alas, the salt water has spoiled most of the contents of these containers and your hunger is not fully sated, but you are thankful for any good fortune at present.

Add 2 points to your Health.

At the end of your search, you spy a small trinket box hidden in some wet clothes in one of the last crates. Opening it, you find some coins, a carved wooden pendant in the shape of a crescent moon representing the god Diana, and several colourless crystals.

Add **5 Denarii**, a **Carved Wooden Diana Pendant [8 Denarii]**, and **7 Clear Crystals [Air]** to your inventory.

Add the codeword **APRON**, then return east the way you came.

Turn to **164**.

95

The venomous spidercrab twitches a few times before its legs curl inwards and it is finally still.

A search of the house yields nothing of interest, the possessions of the previous occupants broken, stolen, or otherwise lost to time.

The sealed empty bottles will allow you to extract some of the spidercrab's venom and preserve for use later. Use an action to apply this venom to a melee weapon during combat or apply it at any time outside combat. Add a +2 modifier to your Weapons ability for the next attack only.

Add **1 Bottle of Spidercrab Venom [Consumable. Weapons +2]** to the consumables section of your inventory. If you have the Zoology skill, your knowledge allows you to extract more of the toxin from the glands and you can add 1 further bottle of venom.

Turn to **124** and mark the House as complete.

96

On the north of the island, the storm has totally receded, leaving a bright blue and cloudless sky. The maelstrom still pounds the lands to the south with an unnatural wall of dark swirling rain marking the border between the two parts of the land.

The air is clear and crisp following the recent rain here and the ground, covered by a thick layer of white pollen, is half sodden even as the warm sun begins drying the dirt.

To continue north to the headland, turn to **50**. To go south to the farm, turn to **141**.

97

You accept the goblet and sniff the contents. It is a deep red wine and has a strong earthy bouquet to it, but you also discern some complex fruit aromas within. You take a sip and enjoy the smooth flavours.

The wine is potent, and you accept just a couple more goblets from them before you pause from a feeling of light-headedness. The lady lights one of the incense sticks protruding from a clay jar and you breathe deeply of the aroma. Its sweet lavender fragrance is pleasant and floral.

Add **Blessing of Somnus [Max Health +1]** to the Powers section of your character sheet. This is a cumulative effect. If you have already received this blessing, amend the description to +2 or +3 as appropriate.

This power increases both your Max Health and Health by 1 point. Also apply this to your companion if you have one.

You chat at length about how the couple survives in such a remote location living off the land, and the old man, several goblets of wine loosening his tongue, offers a cursory explanation. He leans in as if hiding the conversation from a non-existent eavesdropper and whispers.

"Hunting and foraging are easy if you have the right skills and equipment. Finding an abandoned cellar full of wine uses a bit more luck," he chuckles and raises his goblet. You laugh with him at the forthright admission and join him in a toast to good fortune.

Turn to **182**.

98

The cove at which you have arrived has sheer cliffs, looming high above the water and a ragged, rocky beach littered with sharp stones, and tufts of rough vegetation. The sea is calm and the air warm, and you stand facing the cliffs for a few moments to gather your thoughts.

This island is within the Imperial blockade of Sicilia, and no one is aware of your presence here. You are alone and abandoned in this place with no apparent hope of rescue. You will need to explore the land and with your skills, your god's favours, or even fate, you may hope to escape.

Add **Entry 1 - Escape from Phorbantia** to your journal.

About halfway up a steep slope that leads inland, a cave's mouth opens in the cliffside. This offers, after closer inspection, an ideal shelter to rest and dry out your clothes. While the air is quite warm, the sea breeze is still brisk, and you fear you might succumb to the elements if you do not dry your clothes.

The currents have deposited on the shore a long and thin cylindrical length of wood. It could be employed, with some strong wiry grass growing nearby and a small metal blade, to make a spear.

Alternatively, you could dally no longer and risk the elements by continuing inland.

If you still have your **Dagger [Small Melee +0]** in your inventory, and you wish to fashion a spear, turn to **174**.

To take shelter in the cave until your clothes are dry, turn to **33**.

You can head east inland, turn to **63**.

99

Two walls have collapsed into the burned house. You search the soot-covered rubble and find just a few coins scattered among it.

Add **3 Denarii** to your inventory.

During the search, a feeling of lightheaded giddiness overcomes you, and you steady yourself on the blackened wall before you drop to the floor. Nausea and a headache soon replace the grogginess as noxious fumes start to affect you badly.

Make a check against your Physical ability. Add a +1 modifier if you have the Constitution skill.

If you fail to attain at least 1 success, lose 2 points from your Health as you retch and cough uncontrollably.

Turn to **124** and mark the Burned House as complete.

100

Add 1 marker to the time track.

If you have the codeword **YOUTH**, turn to **71**.

The path climbs a windswept hill towards a tall, grey obelisk. Scattered around the pale green and yellow grass lie many shards of flint, useful for lighting fires.

Add **Flint** to your inventory.

As you approach the obelisk, you hear a strange hum and crackling in the air, and note the grass around the base is singed black. It has a series of strange symbols carved into it.

The structure has a badly charred skeleton at its foot, with a few glass beads scattered around it. In the bowl are 5 glass beads.

Before the obelisk is a sculpture of a kneeling human holding aloft a bowl, and beside that, a square container with hundreds of those circular glass balls. It invites you to place beads into the bowl, but how many?

Once you decide how many balls to place, add the amount to this section number and turn to that new section. If you want to put one ball in the bowl for example, turn to section 101.

If that section begins with the text "You place the glass balls into the bowl...", continue reading from that section. Otherwise, a glowing white lightning bolt from the obelisk strikes you, and you must reduce your Health by 8.

You can leave at any time without placing a single bead into the bowl if you wish.

If you wish to go north, turn to **150**. If you want to head south, turn to **32**.

101

The dark black smoke that envelops the island momentarily clears and the warm sun returns.

You take several moments to adjust to your new surroundings. The sound of wildlife is now clear in the air, where mere moments ago they were muted and distant.

As the haze dissipates, thunderous explosions crash to the island's southern region, and you snap back to the moment. These are unmistakably cannon fire, and from the regularity and strength, one or more well-armed ships are discharging all-cannon broadsides.

Smoke rises into the still, clear air over the southern coast, the visible result of the cannons blasting their deadly loads against their hapless enemies. Just three rounds of firing later, and screams replace the sound of cannons as a frantic battle erupts. Lasting mere minutes, they are swiftly silenced.

Tranquillity returns anew, yet so does Sicilia's black smoke, covering the island in a thick choking layer of dust, blocking the sun's light and warmth once again.

Remove any effects that expire at the end of a chapter. Add no further markers to the time track from this point in the volume, and you remain in Chapter III. You may take unlimited rests for the rest of the story as you explore the island at your leisure.

Add the codeword **DEITY** and return to the section you were on.

102

His grin turns to a scowl.

"Bad luck for you then!" The boy burps through his snarl. He looks over at the large group of pirates and takes a breath before shouting for their attention.

You have one brief moment to act. You rapidly wave your hands and promise immediately to get the coins for him. He pauses and smiles to himself, imagining no doubt the wonderful treats he will buy himself.

"Fine", he snorts back "I'll wait here and you bring me my money." He turns to sit on the ship's rail, keeping his guard on the transport.

You retrace your steps unseen back to the cliff side, where you have two options to leave the area.

If you wish to move north, turn to **88**. If you want to proceed west along the southern coast, turn to **6**.

You could also revert to another plan by either talking to the group or even starting a fight.

If you wish to engage them in combat, turn to **65**. If you wish to talk to them, turn to **195**.

103

The size and shape of the holes in the wall, the circular indent, and the angular lines, match that of the stone you obtained from the obelisk on this island. You insert the shape into the first depression and an indistinct flash of white light behind the stone extinguishes as it clicks snugly into place.

Nothing further happens.

Pressing the stone again, it drops out of the hole into your hand. You wonder if the remaining 3 holes need a similar stone for anything further to happen.

You must now leave the cave and return east. Turn to **188**.

104

The path levels off from the steep gradient and the thick jungle canopy is open to the sky. The sun beats down bright, warming rays, and you continue with good speed along this undemanding stretch.

To continue west, turn to **34**. To travel east, turn to **82**.

105

You approach the clearing where you last witnessed the fierce battle between the peregrine alta and the giant beetles. The agitated crashes and roars of the beasts are thunderous and spirited. Both sound very much alive to your ears.

Approaching the treeline with caution, you do indeed see the beasts hungrily pacing around the clearing. Blood splatters, pieces of bone, and scraps of clothing adorn the forest floor. No sign of the alta or the bodies of his comrades remain.

To fight the reptiles, turn to **171**.

If you wish to avoid combat, you can sneak around the clearing or return the way you came. To retreat west, turn to **11**. If you want to exit the clearing southeast towards the coast, turn to **61**.

106

You have cut the pirates' numbers down by over half and, most importantly, this includes their leader. The remaining brigands throw their hands up in the air in surrender, screaming, "Stop! Mercy!" at your ferocious onslaught.

They are genuinely afraid of how swiftly and brutally you have taken them down, and their spirit to fight has utterly vanished.

A boy, barely in his teens, skinny and dirty, approaches you with a thick sword. He seems unstable on his feet and his voice is slurred, perhaps not wholly out of fear considering the barrels of spirits nearby.

"Here," he mumbles with a quivering voice, and holds out a shaking arm. "Take this."

He points to a body on the floor. A large man with a red tunic and long blonde hair.

"You killed the boss. He won't need this now."

Add **Scimitar [Small Melee +2]** to your inventory.

You take the weapon and nod, demonstrating the fight is now over. The boy inches away and continues emptying a small crate of fish into an iron cooking bowl, keeping an eye in your direction. The others warily continue their duties, including disposing of the bodies of their dead comrades in the harbour. They try respectfully to ignore your presence.

Add the codeword **KNAVE**.

Add 4 points to the 🗡 symbol (E) on your character sheet.

Their principal ship, anchored offshore, will soon leave for Neapolis, south of the imperial capital Roma. Travel costs 40 denarii, but shares of any transport profits, or loot from any captured ships on the trip should mitigate this.

They will remain on the island until halfway through Chapter III (indicated by an 'A' on the time track). From that point, you must find another method of escape.

If you stay and wish to exit this area and travel north, turn to **88**. If you want to proceed west along the coast, turn to **6**.

If you have the coin, the time track has not passed midway through Chapter III, and you wish to leave the island now, remove **Entry 1 - Escape from Phorbantia** from your journal if it is active.

Remove **40 Denarii** from your inventory.

Add 5 ability points and spend them on improving any secondary abilities if you wish. Gaining levels in primary abilities requires specialist training and you may not improve these right now.

Add the codeword **INGOT**.

Increase your Health and Prayers to their maximum values, and remove any effects that expire when you leave a volume. Any companion will now depart your service.

Turn to section **344** in Volume I.

107

You walk unhindered along the quiet, salt-swept path. A chaotic breeze blows in every direction, turning the dark mist into a myriad of vortices, swirling erratically around you.

A few more paces and, ahead of you, facing away and barely visible in the turbulence, stands a pale figure. You warily step closer to the statuesque form and realise the white colour is from the bones of a skeleton, upright and waiting. It sways almost imperceptibly on a shattered left leg, its pieces held in place by unknown sorcery.

Sensing your approach, it turns. The clicks of its bones match each movement of its tortured body, and the crunch of the broken leg is most jarring to your ears.

It then stops, utterly motionless, facing you. Then, a small click is all the warning you get as it lifts off from its good leg in a sudden charge. Moving at an incredible pace, it lunges straight at you and, unprepared for the sudden onslaught, you only have time to hold your arms out defensively and brace.

It smashes into you, and you both hit the ground hard. Laying bony fingers around your throat, it attempts to strangle the life from you.

You must now fight this foul creature. As the charge took you by surprise, you must attack unarmed for the first two rounds as you grapple it and struggle to your feet.

The skeleton fights without a weapon and needs a 5 or 6 to hit in combat.

	Weapons	Health	
Skeleton	4	5	

You cannot escape because of the speed of your enemy. This fight is to the death.

If you win and you have the codeword **MINOR**, turn to **31**.

If you win and do not have the codeword **MINOR**, turn to **192**.

108

Powerful waves relentlessly engulf the coastal path, successively ploughing inland and retreating in a violent and rhythmic assault. You remain composed, advancing with speed yet care, moving forward only where the water begins its withdrawal to the sea.

The angry swell rapidly returns to pummel the land after each pull back, but raised outcrops, sporadically located along the way, provide a temporary sanctuary from the immediate environment. The land slopes upwards after a few hundred feet and you proceed onwards.

To move east, turn to **17**. To journey west, turn to **143**.

109

You recognise the shape of the hexagonal stone and it matches the holes where you discovered the cave paintings on this island.

If you have the codeword **BLISS** (Volume III), the codeword **NAVAL** (Volume V), and the codeword **ROYAL** (Volume VIII), **make a note of this section number** and turn to **29**.

You must now leave this area. If you want to travel north, turn to **150**. To progress south, turn to **32**.

110

The path running between the southern bay and the far eastern edge of the island is a dark muddy trail set midway up the steep hills, and some distance from the coastline to the south. Two distinct wooded areas flourish atop the hills, one to the west with dusty golden-brown leaves hanging low on white branches, and eastwards the other with a lush, deep jungle green to them.

In several sections, the path narrows between a sheer climb to one side and a similar drop towards the coast to the other. You take these with great care and they slow you down considerably.

If you have already marked the box below against the current chapter, turn to **54**.

Otherwise, mark the box below against the current chapter and turn to that section number.

Chapter I, turn to **166**. ☐

Chapter II, turn to **149**. ☐

Chapter III, turn to **79**. ☐

111

You enter the wood and at once, distant screaming assaults your senses from all sides. You are unsure if it is the streaming wind, whistling through gnarled and knotted branches, or something more dangerous. The chilling cries grow closer but remain indistinct. They seem to come at you from every direction, yet you see nothing but swaying branches and shaking leaves.

The dense foliage and thick canopy add nothing but more eerie feelings of peril to your continuing journey through this woodland. Ahead, rays of light punch through a thinner layer of the canopy covering a clearing.

The glade is sizeable and home to a strangely coloured tree at its northern side. All other trees in this area are a dark green leafed variety with a deep brown wood, rich in nutrients from the soft, moist ground. The single tree is of a light bark colour with pale beige and white leaves. At many points from the bark, oozes a dark purple sap that seeps down the trunk.

You admire the beauty of this natural scene, yet you are soon aware the soft screaming that followed you through the forest is now replaced with growling and a rustling of leaves.

From the thick bushes stumble three hulking humanoids. Their flesh is pallid and rent with sores and lacerations. From their vicious wounds trickles the same purple sap.

You must fight these monstrosities.

Attacks using the keyword [Aether] cause half damage (rounded down).

Attacks using the keyword [Fire] cause double damage.

	Weapons	Health	
Animated Host	1	4	☐
Animated Host	1	2	☐
Animated Host	1	3	☐

These hapless, lumbering creatures are extraordinarily slow on their feet and you could escape without effort if the fight does not go in your favour. If you wish to flee, add 1 point to the 🜍 symbol (G) on your character sheet. To retreat by the path to the north, turn to **146**. To exit south, turn to **198**.

If you remain in the fight and win, turn to **45**.

112

You mistime a step as you negotiate a small tricky section of the waterlogged path. Slipping on a patch of wet moss, you stumble and badly twist your leg while you collapse to the ground.

Remove 1 point from your Health. You continue your travels, hobbling in pain along the remaining section of the track.

To advance east, turn to **190**. To continue west, turn to **88**.

113

The rain has turned the fields into a boggy mire, with standing pools of water growing wide and deep in the deluge. Semi eaten crops are piled high and amazes you how much of a pest problem this farmer has.

Rustling from several uneaten lines of crops is an early sign that not only does the farmer have a pest problem, but now you have as well. Several sharp-toothed rodents, some the size of a domesticated cat launch themselves at you, an insatiable hunger burning in their eyes.

You must now fight these ravenous creatures.

Each field rat's bite is painful and damaging, but they are relatively small and weak creatures. Each rat's damage is halved, rounding down to the nearest whole number. A field rat, therefore, needs to roll a success on both combat dice to score a single hit.

Due to their small size, all field rats can perform a melee attack in a combat round. You and any companions or allies can also attack any of them in melee combat.

	Weapons	Health	
Large Field Rat	2	2	☐
Large Field Rat	2	2	☐
Large Field Rat	2	2	☐
Small Field Rat	2	1	☐
Small Field Rat	2	1	☐
Small Field Rat	2	1	☐
Small Field Rat	2	1	☐

You can escape at any time. If so, take one last attack from each remaining enemy as you flee and add 1 point to the 🐾 symbol (G) on your character sheet. To escape and continue north to the farm, turn to **141**. To go south to the T junction, turn to **68**.

If you win the combat, turn to **183**.

114

Legionaries are busy freeing slaves and clearing up contraband, weapons, and bodies of rough looking individuals, likely brigands or pirates of some sort, in the aftermath of an intense and bloody battle. They accept, with the confirmation of several malnourished captives, you are not one of the criminals, and you are free to enter the camp or leave as you wish.

They offer to give you and any companion passage off the island to their next destination. Their ship will be here for several days, so you can continue exploring the island as much as you wish.

You may continue to explore the island. If you wish to do so and go north, turn to **88**. If you wish to head west along the south coast of the island, turn to **6**.

The navy is heading to Neapolis, south of Roma, the imperial capital. They understand the pirates have an established trade link to that city and need to investigate.

If you want to leave now, remove **Entry 1 - Escape from Phorbantia** from your journal if it is active.

Add 5 ability points and spend them on improving any secondary abilities if you wish. Gaining levels in primary abilities requires specialist training and you may not improve these right now. You may save any unused points for later.

Increase your Health and Prayers to their maximum values, and remove any effects that expire when you leave a volume. Any companion will now depart your service.

Turn to section **695** in Volume I.

115

Your short travel through the open brush starts uneventfully, and the bright spring air makes the walk quite a pleasant endeavour. The wind from the coast hits the island in brief gusts and the bushes and shrubs sway with vigour, dislodging pollen in heavy white clouds above the ground. The wind dies down eventually, and the pollen hangs thick in the still air.

Brushing away the larger grains that tickle and irritate your face, you spit smaller specks from your mouth, which are only replaced at once by further dust.

Your eyes start to water, your nose streams, and you choke as the thick powder fills your lungs, nose, and throat.

Lose 2 Health as you struggle to make your way through the pollen-stuffed air. Thankfully, the sudden bloom covers a compact area and you briskly escape.

To resume your progress north to the headland, turn to **50**. To journey south to the farm, turn to **141**.

116

You sit on the chair and the relief on your body as you sink into the cushion is immediate and satisfying. A warming sensation passes through your limbs as the exertions of your time on this island unwind and disappear.

Add **Blessing of Somnus [Max Health +1]** to the Powers section of your character sheet. This is a cumulative effect. If you have already received this blessing, amend the description to +2 or +3 as appropriate.

This power increases both your Max Health and Health by 1 point. Also apply this to your companion if you have one.

"What brings you to this out-of-the-way place?" The lady asks, and you chat about your arrival here. They explain they came to the island months ago to escape from the chaos of "imperial subjugation" as they refer to it, with more than an irritated tone.

"We do like the peace and quiet, but we have missed civilised conversations." The elderly gentleman looks somewhat sad by this as he checks the pot while remembering old friendships.

"That might just be ready," he chirpily remarks and produces some wooden bowls.

He ladles out two bowls from the pot and looks at you. "Would you like some venison stew?"

If you take him up on his offer for food, turn to **15**.

If not, turn to **179**.

117

Add 1 marker to the time track.

You stand at the edge of the shore and the gentle waves lap in the shallow waters. A small islet, less than one hundred paces in length, sits a short wade out to sea. A rocky outcrop that appears, at first glance, barren and devoid of anything of interest or value.

If you have the codeword **LUCID**, turn to **69**.

If you have the codeword **OUTER**, turn to **172**.

Otherwise, you spend some time searching the island, which does indeed lack anything to interest to you at present. You return northeast to the junction. Turn to **143**.

118

Add 1 marker to the time track.

You descend the steep, narrow path that runs in a jagged line down the cliffs to a cove with a rocky beach at the shoreline.

If you have the codeword **URBAN**, turn to **19**.

If you have the codeword **APRON**, turn to **185**.

If you are on Chapter II or Chapter III of the time track, turn to **94**.

Otherwise, the path ends at a cove with a rocky sandstone beach. There is nothing for you here, so you must return east. Turn to **164**.

119

If you are on Chapter III of the time track, turn to **64**.

Your journey along the road is remarkably pleasant, and you make excellent progress, untroubled by any dangers.

Interestingly, however, you now spot that a circular depression in the landscape, roughly 30 to 40 feet in diameter, has appeared since you last travelled this route. The earth is churned and broken, and leafy branches reach upwards from a tree swallowed by the rough ground.

To proceed north, turn to **34**. To move south, turn to **88**.

120

The snaking path is as you remember it from your recent traversal, and your journey along its relatively short length is quickened from your prior knowledge.

To progress west towards the coast, turn to **85**. To head east up the mountain, turn to **133**.

121

The dark mist covering the area mutes the colour tones between the rocks and the plants. The shrubs are wilted and stiff, motionless even with an occasional warm gust of wind. You make your way along the path with ease.

To travel north, turn to **100**. To go south, turn to **143**.

122

The jungle canopy hangs thick and low above your head and the buzz of thousands of tiny insects hum incessantly. The path is wide, yet the plants encroach on many parts and several times you must push your way hard through thicker, more overgrown sections.

At one such point, you push a branch hard until it snaps. A similar snap from your left accompanies a low growl from within the dense bushes.

In an instant, a giant two-headed cat, vibrant green and yellow stripes decorate its fur and two maws full of razor-sharp fangs, jumps out and puts you flat on your back. One head hisses, eyes looking straight at you with a violent ferocity, its teeth bared and whiskers twitching. The other head roars to the heavens before coming down hard, mouth open, ready to feed.

Lose 2 from your Health as it embeds its claws into your back, and its dagger-like teeth from one head bites hard into your shoulder.

	Weapons	Health	
Duo Tigris	3	2	

You cannot escape as the tigris will easily chase you down and rip you apart as you flee.

If you win, turn to **160**.

123

"First, a test of your tongue. Tell us your story." He demands.

He is assessing your background and your demeanour to see if you are of the right kind to join the group.

Make a check against your Social ability. Add a +1 modifier each if you have the Deception, Intimidation, Persuasion, or Streetwise skills. In addition, you earn a +3 modifier if the total of the ⑨ symbol (A) on your character sheet is 8 or greater.

If you gain at least 2 successes, note that you passed this test and turn to **60**.

124

Several buildings have not fully collapsed, offering an excellent opportunity to explore the abandoned village.

A substantial villa stands on the western edge overlooking the square. The paint long since peeled and weathered away, it still remains an imposing sight, dominating the settlement by its sheer expanse.

To the south, adjoining the path that exits the village through a heavily forested area of golden-brown trees, is a tall, narrow barn.

On the eastern boundary of the town, a cobbled road leads from the village into another thick, wooded area, this one with verdant, dark green foliage. Bounding this road on each side stand two houses. One is in excellent condition considering its age, and the other is a charred and burned wreck, defiantly standing tall despite its condition.

A third cobbled road leads north into another treeline where it gradates into a dirt track.

To the west, the imposing foothills and mountains that run down the western flank of the island rise high above the treetops. The lighter-coloured trees to the southern half merge into the mid-green hue that marks the northern trees. There are piles of droppings, dozens in number, and several small trails leading into the dense treeline where, you suspect, the animals responsible watch with care, waiting eagerly for your departure.

If you have ticked the box below against a building to show it is complete, you may not revisit that area again. Do not mark a location complete until the text instructs you to.

To explore the villa, turn to **56**. ☐

To explore the barn, turn to **75**. ☐

To explore the house, turn to **173**. ☐

To explore the burned house, turn to **99**. ☐

If you have attained at least level 1 in the Mystical ability, you recognise the purpose of the ruined fountain. Feeling around under the surface of the brown water, your hand passes over several lumps on the stone. Prying one out, and washing the hardened grime from the surface, the soft blue glow of a water crystal greets you. The liquid within the bowl bubbles and the water level lowers further.

There are **12 Blue Crystals [Water]** remaining in the fountain, and you may take as many as you wish. If you do not remove all crystals, note how many remain below. You can return to collect others at a later point.

```
┌─────────────────┐
│                 │
└─────────────────┘
```

You may not take any of these hidden crystals unless you have at least level 1 in the

Mystical ability. To the untrained eye, they are mere bumps on a bowl submerged in the dark water.

If you wish to leave the village and head north, turn to **198**.

To journey east, turn to **11**.

To move south, turn to **156**.

125

You complete the short distance in good time, confident if you return with the same weather conditions, you will traverse the slopes without difficulty, remembering both the safe and difficult routes along the path.

To climb west to the mountain peak, turn to **133**. To descend northeast to the crossroads, turn to **59**.

126

There is silence among the group. The captain tongues his teeth, trying to remove a piece of meat from between them as he decides your fate. You know your performance was poor, and the leader soon agrees with your thoughts.

"Put this cargo in chains." He orders and several grinning bandits move towards you.

You waste no time in lunging to attack, and the speed of your assault catches the brigands off-guard, taking them altogether by surprise. Turn to **65**.

127

You watch the skies which show no signs of cloud or storms, yet the crackling and tingling remain.

Abruptly, a single bolt of blue lightning shoots forth from the ground. Passing close enough for you to smell the metallic burning, it likewise singes your skin and hair as it strikes upwards.

Roll one die and lose that amount of Health. This is the equivalent of a single combat attack, and the damage is reduced by armour, agility, or other items and powers as it would be in combat.

You collapse forward and sprint through the clearing as several more strikes punch up into the blue sky. If you were not so quick to run, your journey would doubtless have ended here.

To escape west, turn to **34**. To flee east, turn to **82**.

128

Their small rusty blades and patchwork armour are of inferior quality and offer no use to you. Luckily, the sinapis ferocis are keen on shiny and interesting objects, and one has a pouch secreted in a flap of leather with a small amount of coin within.

Add **4 Denarii** to your inventory.

To continue west towards the coast, turn to **85**. Continue east up the mountain, turn to 133.

129

If you have the codeword **YOUTH** (From this volume), the codeword **BLISS** (Volume III), the codeword **NAVAL** (Volume V), and the codeword **ROYAL** (Volume VIII), **make a note of this section number** and turn to **29**.

You are at the bottom of a rocky cavern bathed in natural light. The opening is 20 feet above your head and a rope hangs down to the floor, secured to an overhanging tree precariously teetering at the edge of the rim. Stones and fresh soil drop every so often to the floor, and it appears this hole has only recently opened.

The faint purple glow from the circular window set into the grey rock behind you marks your entry into this land. Whichever land this might be.

The symbol of interlinked hexagonal shapes embossed on this surface differs from the image you observed on the reverse of the window.

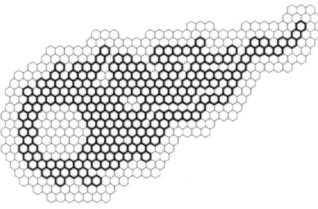

Climbing the rope, you pull yourself from the hole and take in your surroundings.

You stand by a quiet woodland path. The trees on either side of the cobbled road, running straight through the wood, are a mix of tones with vibrant golden leaves swaying gently on muted pale yellow, almost white branches.

A deep rumbling startles you from behind, and you spin around sharply. As you do, you witness the tree, and then the sinkhole's edges collapse in on itself. Your return is now blocked.

There is a wide border between the road and the tree line, with pale and dead-looking grass swaying in the wind. The compass shows the road runs north to south and you consider your next move as, in the near distance, you see a fresh sinkhole open. This area is geologically active and you may not wish to linger.

If you want to progress north, turn to **34**. If you would like to advance south, turn to **88**.

130

Add the codeword **BENCH**.

The peregrine alta catches his breath. "Much gratitude, stranger. I could not have survived this on my own." He gasps between deep breaths. "I am Regulus. Lecturer in the Collegia Mysticum in Roma, and support to the Eighth Indomita Legion."

He pauses once again to remove his helmet. He strokes his bald head and frowns.

"You are obviously a very capable individual, and my employment has now ended." He motions to the corpses of the legionaries.

"It would honour me to join you in your travels on this island, else I will remain here and contemplate."

If you wish to add Regulus as a companion, turn to the back of this volume, where you will find his details. Add these to the companion section of your character sheet and your current companion will head back to their usual location.

If Regulus joins you, add the codeword **GRADE**.

Regulus will accompany you for no cost while you remain in this volume. He will depart from your service should you leave the volume.

If you do not wish him to accompany you, he will remain in this area. You can return at any point to employ his services.

You must now leave the clearing. If you wish to go west towards the centre of the island, turn to **11**. If you wish to head southeast towards the eastern coast, turn to **61**.

131

You kick off towards the raft. Beginning with strong momentum, your progress swiftly falters in the choppy waters. Your armour, sodden and heavy, drags on you with each stroke and you are soon being pulled under the surface by the weight. To add to the threat, several triple-finned fan sharks eagerly circle you, curious of your splashing.

In serious danger of drowning, you unbuckle your armour, which straight away drops out of sight on its journey to the sea floor, and furiously swim with renewed vigour once again towards the raft.

Remove **Leather Brigandine [Light Armour +1]** from your inventory

The extra impetus this provides ensures your last breath will not be of the salty Mediterranean water, but is not enough to elude the hungry creatures within.

You feel a painful jolt to your leg as one of the fan sharks embeds its serrated teeth deep into your flesh. It remains latched on hard, and you struggle and thrash in the water as it pulls you across the surface.

Make a check against your Physical ability. Add a +1 modifier each if you have the Strength or Swimming skills.

If you achieve at least 1 success, turn to **155**. If not, turn to **80**.

132

You crawl along the floor, edging forward by the inch, between a stack of empty wooden crates. Thrown atop one another, they waver in the breeze with the lack of weight.

Their haphazard arrangement makes it difficult to judge the gaps, and one proves to be smaller than you had expected. Your elbow clumsily brushes the corner of a crate.

The entire stack topples and crashes to the floor, leaving you lying prone on the stone ground in full view of the astonished pirates.

They look at you, open-mouthed in disbelief, and you spend a few moments staring at each other in this strange and vaguely comical situation. The calm is soon to evaporate.

You have a tiny window of time to escape, and the brigands won't waste their time chasing down one lone interloper. There are two options open to leave the area before they get to you. If you wish to flee north, turn to **88**. If you want to escape west along the southern coast, turn to **6**.

Otherwise, you charge at pace towards the pirates and engage in combat.

Turn to **65**.

133

Add 1 marker to the time track.

If you have the codeword **HALVE**, turn to **67**. If not, turn to **184**.

134

Feeling weary and dizzy, your muscles ache as if you had hiked across the island for days without rest. In your jumbled mind, you still sense a spark of familiarity with this uncanny situation.

"Please sit down," the old man beckons.

You are unsteady on your feet, and you almost collapse from the blood draining from your head.

"What brings you to this out-of-the-way place?" the lady asks. You do not respond.

"We do like the peace and quiet, but we have missed civilised conversations." The elderly gentleman looks somewhat sad by this as he checks the pot.

"That might be ready," he says as he produces some wooden bowls.

He ladles out two bowls from the pot and looks at you. "Would you like some venison stew?"

A shard of memory momentarily returns, and you hold out your palm, firmly replying. "No!"

The man then produces three silver goblets and a tall, thin bottle of red liquid.

"Would you join us in a glass of wine?" he instead offers.

You step back further, and the couple stand in unison snarling and spitting.

"SIT DOWN!" they both scream in unnatural and inhuman echoes. Their eyes glow a bright, fiery green in the darkness.

That finally convinces you to escape from this place with haste. Running past the dead rat that lies rotten and maggot-ridden on the branch, you realise it is dawn again. Your sore body and muddled thoughts make it feel you have been here for days without food or rest.

Add markers to the time track equal to the total value recorded against the Max Health modifier from the **Blessing of Somnus** on your character sheet. That is one marker each for sitting down, eating the stew, and taking the wine.

Remove **Blessing of Somnus** from your character sheet and reduce your Max Health and Health by the value of the modifier. These should match the values immediately before you arrived at this location.

Lose that number *again* from your Health. You are now starving, dehydrated and deprived of sleep. If you have the Infernals skill, or if you have the patron god keyword of [Infernal] and use 1 Prayer, ignore this second loss of Health. Your knowledge and favour of the dark gods and their servants' methods have saved you *this time*.

Repeat the above for any companion travelling with you.

Add the codeword **WAVER**.

To escape northwest to the crossroads, turn to **59**. To go southeast towards the Y junction, turn to **198**.

135

Add 1 marker to the time track.

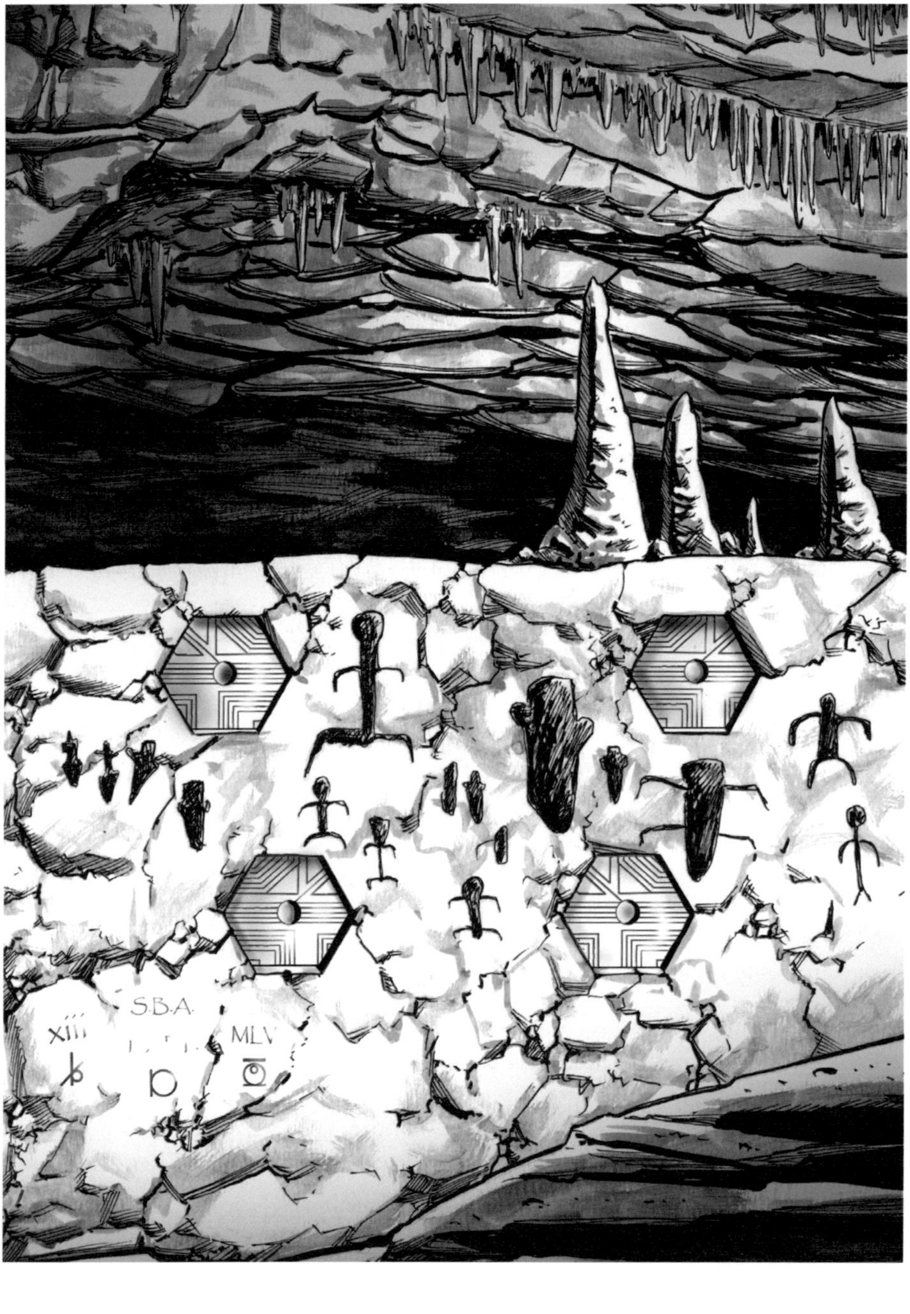

Add the codeword **PINCH**.

You pass down a narrow path that drops steeply towards the rocky shoreline before turning back inland to a large cave beneath the starkly coloured and oppressive cliff face. Within the cave, you struggle in the dusty gloom to make out strange markings on the wall.

Painted in a deep black ink, stylised images of humans, animals, and other shapes adorn the cave walls. Art from a bygone era, likely even pre-dating the Fire by millennia.

You note four shallow hexagonal-shaped recesses set into the wall with a further smaller circular hole in the centre of those. Angular lines run from each edge of the hollows.

Someone's initials are carved into the wall above what appears to be a date. The thirteenth day of an indistinctly carved month, in the year IA1055.

If you have the codeword **VAGUE**, turn to **81**.

If you have the codeword **CABAL**, turn to **41**.

If you have the codeword **YOUTH**, turn to **103**.

Otherwise, there is nothing else for you here and you must return east. Turn to **188**.

136

Add the codeword **JEWEL**.

The last of the wolves vanishes in a sparkling blue and brilliant white plume of smoke and you catch your breath after the hard fought battle. The heavy wooden door of the farmhouse opens a little, someone briefly checking why the howling and baying has halted. It then fully opens to reveal the inhabitants.

Two ghostly forms of an elderly man and woman take you aback as they exit the building, fearfully glancing around for danger. They realise their tormentors exist no more, and the man collapses to his knees, sobbing.

"Thank you, kind stranger." The woman says, her voice a curious tone, faintly distant and echoing. "I cannot remember the last time there was quiet."

You sense relief in the air as peace and tranquillity returns, and you can only guess how long this scene has played out.

The man rises back to his feet and ushers you into the house. "Please, come in and help yourself to food, wine, and a comfortable bed. You earned it."

You walk into an immaculate farmhouse. Fresh meat and fish hang drying from the rafters, and ripe vegetables sit nicely arranged in baskets. The bed has a simple straw mattress covered by furs and, while not luxurious, will provide you with restful and safe slumber.

Both ghostly farmers leave you alone as they tend to the fields. Once you have taken any respite and sustenance you need, you must leave the comforts of the house and continue your journey.

If you wish to head towards the northernmost headland of the island, turn to **177**. To return south back into the central region, turn to **43**.

137

The treacherous conditions on the path combined with the low light cause you to stumble and your feet dislodge a large stone. Your ankle twists, almost sending you hurtling down a steep drop with a shower of dirt and rocks. Punching your arm forward, you grab a protruding bush which saves you from an unfortunate and painful fall.

Inching forward, you take the utmost care following your recent near miss. This caution is rewarded, and you negotiate the rest of this difficult section without issue. Soon you are on your way at a calm strolling pace along the more forgiving closing stretch.

To continue east, turn to **190**. To travel west, turn to **88**.

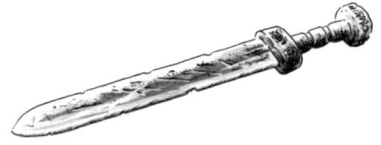

138

You approach the island of Phorbantia from the northwest and the ship sails as close to a small, sheltered bay as the jagged rocks, protruding like claws from the waters, will allow.

The crew lower a rowboat into the calm waters, and you climb aboard to proceed to the rugged beach ahead.

You relax with the tranquillity of the calm air and flat seas, but the black pillar of smoke rising without end from Sicilia reminds you to always be on your guard in this place. The strange effects of its unknown power are numerous and almost exclusively dangerous.

The island's topography is wholly unsuitable for any method of travelling apart from on foot. You may not use items with the keyword of [Land Transport] in your exploration of the island.

If you have the codeword **YOUTH** (From this volume), the codeword **BLISS** (Volume III), the codeword **NAVAL** (Volume V), and the codeword **ROYAL** (Volume VIII), **make a note of this section number** and turn to **29**.

Turn to **189**.

139

You look up at the mountain as you pass the northern face and glimpse the nest's edge atop its peak. All is peaceful in the air, but you glimpse a small, fleeting movement on the nest's edge. It was quick and indistinct, yet you are certain you spotted a small wing hanging over the side.

To head southwest to a T junction, turn to **188**. To go southeast to a crossroads, turn to **59**.

140

If you **do not** have the codeword **MINOR**, turn to **57**.

Otherwise, the empty path offers nothing of interest to you.

To descend west to the sea, turn to **118**. To continue east towards a T junction, turn to **68**.

141

Add 1 marker to the time track.

If you have the codeword **JEWEL**, turn to **83**. Otherwise, turn to **21**.

142

The pirates laugh and jovially banter about the brawl they just witnessed. They give you a few minutes to recover from the ordeal, but it is soon time for your next test.

They drag one of the slaves from the group, a naked man, thin and sickly from his imprisonment. He is chained by both hands and feet, and is thrown unceremoniously to the leader's feet, who hands you a flintlock pistol.

"We need people who can shoot straight in the heat of battle." He points to the slave in front of him, shivering and sobbing with fear. "This cargo here has already escaped twice. This time will be its last."

He unshackles the scrawny man and shouts, "Run!" to which the hapless prisoner obeys.

The man sprints towards the path leading up the cliffs. He is fast, surprising considering his condition, but the body can perform remarkable feats given the right circumstances. He weaves and ducks, expecting your shot at any moment. The pirates again chortle heartily, and you have just seconds to take your shot.

The leader now has his back to you, watching the fleeing captive with tremendous amusement. He is off-guard. You have a brief window of opportunity and you cannot miss him at this distance. If you wish to fire on the captain, remembering there are a dozen pirates in the group near you, turn to **194**.

Otherwise, make a ranged attack using your Weapons ability with a +0 modifier from the weapon you are handed. Roll no dice and purposefully miss if you do not wish to kill the prisoner.

If you succeed by causing at least 1 damage with the shot, turn to **168**.

If you fail, either on purpose, or down to bad luck, turn to **30**.

143

You are at T junction.

To the southwest, the path drops to a rocky beach with a tiny, barren island just offshore. The sea is a light sapphire colour, shallow yet quite choppy, and you could try to wade or swim out to it.

North, the path follows the westerly coast of the island, and to the east, it hugs the southern coast.

To proceed southwest to the small island, turn to **117**. If you wish to head north, turn to **32**. If you would like to travel east, turn to **6**.

144

With confidence and purpose, you make your way along the route you navigated before, in these exact conditions with no problems. The going, while demanding, is familiar to an experienced traveller like yourself.

To continue west, turn to **133**. To go northeast, turn to **59**.

145

The last of your enemies fall, and you catch your breath before continuing your journey. A search of the bodies results in nothing other than a trio of large, beautifully coloured Aer volatis feathers. Two feet in length, they have a dark brown base that gradates to light brown, then white towards the tip where it ends in a striking red point.

Add **3 Aer Volatis Feathers [6 Denarii]** to your inventory. This is the total value, and they are worth 2 denarii each if you do not wish to sell them all.

To resume your journey north, turn to **85**. To proceed south, turn to **100**.

146

You are at a fork in the path at a Y junction deep within the thick forest.

Northwards, the dirt trail passes through the woodland and drops to another junction close by. Southwest, the path leads to a sparsely forested area that grows below the highest peak on the island. In the southeast, a winding trail enters a dark oppressive wood with a thick canopy and overgrown brush.

If you wish to travel north, turn to **68**. To journey southwest towards the mountain, turn to **59**. To advance southeast to the dark wood, turn to **24**.

147

You creep onto the boat, out of sight of the crew on shore, and stow yourself aboard in the supply pantry. Stacked to the ceiling, it is full of crates, barrels, and sacks, and you find a concealed spot to hide.

If the time track has passed midway through Chapter III (denoted by an 'A' on the track), you soon realise the boat will not depart the island for weeks. This means of escape is no longer possible, as they would eventually discover you before leaving. You must change your approach.

To abandon your hiding place and engage them in combat, turn to **65**. If you wish to talk to them, turn to **195**. To leave this area and move north, turn to **88**. If you wish to leave and head west along the southern coast, turn to **6**.

If the Time Track has not passed midway through Chapter III, and you wish to leave the island now, then the boy stays true to his word. Any companion creeps aboard late at night to join you and remains hidden for the duration.

A day later, after a quick journey out of the bay and into the Mediterranean itself, you sneak aboard the main galleon from the transport unnoticed with his assistance.

Packed with cargo, the large vessel offers many concealed places to stow away during the voyage. You rest, eat and sleep in relative comfort during this time, untroubled by the unsuspecting brigands you share the journey with.

Add 5 ability points and spend them on improving any secondary abilities if you wish. Gaining levels in primary abilities requires specialist training and you may not improve these right now. You may save any unused points for later.

Add the codeword **INGOT**,

Remove **Entry 1 - Escape from Phorbantia** from your journal if it is active.

Increase your Health and Prayers to their maximum values, and remove any effects that expire when you leave a volume. Any companion will now depart your service.

Turn to section **481** in Volume I.

148

The black skies are still and you struggle to distinguish clouds from the smoke, it is so thick and suffocating in places. There have been no signs of lightning or thunder since the previous storm subsided, yet the tingling on your skin grows ever stronger.

Behind you, a single electric blue lance of lightning erupts from the ground. With the brightness, even dulled by the smoke, your shadow casts a clear silhouette in the smog ahead. Searing pain then rips up your back.

Roll one die and lose that amount of Health. This is the equivalent of a single combat attack, and the damage is reduced by armour, agility, or other items and powers as it would be in combat.

This unexpected blast takes you aback, and you spin to dive out of the clearing as several other powerful bolts strike upwards at the forest canopy.

Make two checks against your Agility ability. For each check that you fail to gain at least 1 success against, take a further attack with 1 die of damage from these additional blasts.

To retreat west, turn to **34**. To go east, turn to **82**.

149

The path has been turned gravely treacherous by the storms, and the rocks threaten to trip and confound your every step. Many hidden dangers cover the dark, wet rocks, and more than once, your foot slips on some unseen plant life pasted flat against a black, shining surface.

Make a check against your Agility ability. Add a +1 modifier if you have the Night

Vision skill to aid you in spotting these slippery dangers.

If you accomplish at least 1 success, turn to **25**. If you fail, turn to **112**.

150

The path is narrow and set back a good distance from the coast, hugging the base of the central peaks along its length. The ground is level and sparse with vegetation, making your progress easy.

If you have already marked the box below against the current chapter, turn to **26**.

Otherwise, mark the box below against the current chapter and turn to that section number.

Chapter I, turn to **13**.

Chapter II, turn to **49**.

Chapter III, turn to **186**.

151

Add 1 marker to the time track.

If you have the codeword **TREAD**, turn to **55**.

You descend the short distance to sea level in the bay and survey the landscape. Cliffs to the northeastern edge provide excellent protection from the worst of the weather Sicilia can muster. The waters are calm, and near the mouth of the bay, the top of a mast protrudes at an odd angle from the clear waters.

A ship, a frigate from the central fleet, lies collapsed and broken on the rocks that jut above the surface. A single sail wavers in the wind on the broken mast, several ropes preventing it from hitting the water, so the wreck likely is only likely a week old.

If you currently have, or can gain now, the **Water Breathing** power and you want to explore the wreck, turn to **47**.

Otherwise, you leave the bay and climb the gentle hill northwest. Turn to **190**.

152

Add 3 markers to the time track.

You dive at the barrel and closely hug it on the side furthest from the keen eyes on the naval ships, giving yourself as best a chance as possible to evade their gaze. Kicking your feet below the water, you make slow and painful progress in escaping the area, and the distant island never seems to approach closer. Thankfully, because of the relative distances, the nearby naval ships get more distant with time and at least you know you are making progress, albeit at a paddling pace.

In that instant, something brushes against your leg, almost causing you to lose your grip on the barrel. Then, a sharp pain tears down your right calf and you kick back instinctively, hitting nothing.

Lose 2 Health.

You decide floating by the barrel is now no longer an option and are aware that several other pieces of flotsam join you in your slow progress to the island. You may have caught some luck, or your favoured god may this time have favoured you. It seems you are in a current leading you straight to your destination.

Using the dagger, you pry open the barrel. Bundles of a strange-smelling, bright pink moss pour into the sea, floating wide on the waters from your position. The barrel is large enough to climb comfortably in and hide from sight of any curious ships.

You check your legs for injuries. There is a single puncture wound in your calf and mercifully very little bleeding.

You then settle down for the journey, popping your head from the barrel, occasionally checking for pursuers. None follow and you float for an entire day unhindered before being deposited near the shore of a rocky beach on the island.

Turn to **98**.

153

Rains lash the coast hard and the lightning strikes are worryingly close, but the trail is well preserved, and you advance with little difficulty.

To progress southeast, turn to **190**. To continue northwest, turn to **82**.

154

The clearing where you fought and won against the giant beetles is now a tranquil oasis of calm, a stark contrast to your first visit, and you pass through without incident. The bodies are gone, dragged into the undergrowth by scavengers to be consumed at leisure. These scavengers, at least, are aware of the safer spots to feed.

If you wish to exit the clearing and travel west, turn to **11**. If you wish to head southeast, turn to **61**.

155

You writhe and twist, struggling to kick the shark loose. It rips a small yet painful chunk of skin and flesh away from your leg, but you are otherwise unharmed. You continue swimming to the raft at a much more hurried pace.

Turn to **42**.

156

The trail cuts its way downhill from the centre of the island, as a meandering river would flow to the sea, ending at the southerly coast. The woods on either side are a mix of their tones, with vibrant golden leaves swaying on muted pale yellow and white branches.

A wide border between the cobbled path and the thin treeline is home to long, almost dead-looking grass moving stiffly in the gentle wind.

If you have already marked the box below against the current chapter, turn to **119**.

Otherwise, mark the box below against the current chapter and turn to that section number.

Chapter I, turn to **181**. ☐

Chapter II, turn to **197**. ☐

Chapter III, turn to **64**. ☐

157

🌿☐☐

The thick leaves of these bushes are plump and glistening, well-nourished by the recent rains.

If you have the Herbalism skill, you may use some rare leaves that flourish in patches to make an instant healing balm with no equipment or other ingredients. Add **1 Healing Balm [Consumable. Health +5]** to the consumables section of your inventory, if so.

To continue north, turn to **100**. To continue south, turn to **143**.

158

You approach a pair of large boulders that half block the path, a small gap between them allowing snug passage onwards.

Four skeletons, shining bright white even in the darkened landscape, lie broken on the dirt. They are bipedal and diminutive, only four feet tall, with strangely shaped wide skulls that sport long sharp teeth. On some of the broken bones, cuts and clean breaks are evidence these resulted from combat.

Small scraps of flesh still hang off the bones. These unfortunate creatures were fed upon very recently.

To continue west towards the coast, turn to **85**. To ascend the mountain eastwards, turn to **133**.

159

The pirates acknowledge you on your approach and continue with their work. Unless you wish to leave the island or rest, there is nothing further of interest here now.

If you want to exit the area and go north, turn to **88**. If you wish to move west along the coast, turn to **6**.

If you have 40 denarii for passage, the time track has not passed midway through Chapter III, denoted by the letter 'A' on the track, and you wish to leave the island now, remove **Entry 1 - Escape from Phorbantia** from your journal if it is active.

Add 5 ability points and spend them on improving any secondary abilities if you wish. Gaining levels in primary abilities requires specialist training and you may not improve these now. You may save any unused points for later.

Remove **40 Denarii** from your inventory

Add the codeword **INGOT**.

Increase your Health and Prayers to their maximum values, and remove any effects that expire when you leave a volume. Any companion will now depart your service.

Turn to section **344** in Volume I.

160

The beast is dead.

If you have a **Dagger** or **Knife** in your inventory, you may skin the dead animal for its pelt, which is sure to fetch a fine price with any merchant.

If so, and you have the Hunting skill, add **2 Uncommon Hides** to the resources section of your character sheet. Without the Hunting skill, add **2 Common Hides**.

You may now continue safely on your way.

To resume your travels southeast, turn to **190**. To continue northwest, turn to **82**.

161

You place the glass balls into the bowl and the symbols on the obelisk abruptly glow intensely bright and then fade just as quickly.

Add the codeword **YOUTH**.

A momentary click follows, and a hexagonal stone set into the lower part of the obelisk, drops down and lands on the plinth. The mysterious tablet is thin, roughly the size of your hand, with a smaller circular knob protruding from the back.

Several angular lines run across the stone's rear from one edge to another, but there are no clues to what its function might offer.

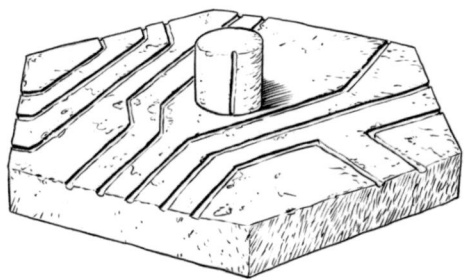

Add **Mysterious Hexagonal Stone** to your inventory.

If you have the codeword **PINCH**, turn to **109**.

If you have the codeword **BLISS** (Volume III), the codeword **NAVAL** (Volume V), and the codeword **ROYAL** (Volume VIII), **make a note of this section number** and turn to **29**.

You must now leave this area. If you want to head north, turn to **150**. To proceed south, turn to **32**.

162

The shark dives in for its attack, and yanking your body aside, you are quick and fortunate enough that its head glances harmlessly off your thigh. Diving deep below the waves, your attacker, more suited to hunting targets on or near the surface, turns its attention to the scores of less able victims presented to it.

Breaching the surface two minutes later, you gasp for air, but otherwise unharmed. You continue at pace with your approach to the island.

Turn to **51**.

163

The rain has saturated the mud, and the rocks come loose easily from the sodden dirt. Gripping hold of a large stone embedded deep into the rock face, you use it to bear a good load of your weight as you swing from one foothold to another.

It is, alas, more weight than the rock can bear. It dislodges from its less than solid foundation, and you both fall several feet to an outcrop below. You land hard on your back and the rock slams into your leg. Nothing is broken, but you will be hobbling for a few hours on your badly swelled ankle.

Lose 2 Health. If you currently have the **Feather** or **Flight** power, or the Reflexes skill, only lose 1 Health as the fall was mitigated. The rock, however, still inflicted painful damage.

The fall is so sudden that if you have neither power nor the skill, you cannot react in time to gain a benefit from an item or other means.

To resume your climb west to the mountain peak, turn to **133**. To journey northeast to the crossroads, turn to **59**.

164

The wide path is sparse with vegetation, and any plants or shrubs you do spot are withered and colourless. A strong salty breeze sweeps up from the sea, bleaching the exposed stones a dazzling white.

If you have already marked the box below against the current chapter, turn to **31**.

Otherwise, mark the box below against the current chapter and turn to that section number.

Chapter I, turn to **57**. ☐

Chapter II, turn to **140**. ☐

Chapter III, turn to **107**. ☐

165

Add the codeword **TREAD**.

The last eel twitches as it sinks in the red water to the wooden floor of the deck. Splinters and fragments of wood float from several of the crates smashed apart in your struggle. Dozens of small glass bottles, a thick black liquid contained within, float upwards to the surface.

Some bottles have been shattered, spilling the inky liquid into the water. The oily slick clings to your skin and clothing as you search the rest of the shipwreck, but you find nothing else of interest. Grabbing a bottle, you exit the wreck and swim back to shore.

You climb the beach and observe the bay. Many of the bottles now bob in the gentle waters, having broken free from the ship.

Add **Bottle of Oil [Consumable]** to your inventory.

You then leave the bay on the only available path to the northwest.

Turn to **190**.

166

The track through this area of the island is rugged and difficult to traverse. Rocks slip on the steep hilly banks, but you keep your footing helped by the bright and warm day. More inclement weather would soon cause this stretch to become a hazardous threat to your health, but you are fortunate enough to enjoy the clear and dry conditions at this moment.

To proceed east, turn to **190**. To continue west, turn to **88**.

167

If you have the codeword **WAVER**, turn to **3**.

The path passes between two separate wooded areas that enjoy a bright green spring canopy on each side.

The grassland is lush and verdant, and trees encroach on the path, frequently providing a small amount of shelter.

At a tight turn in the path, your approach startles a hawk perched on a branch, which flies off with an angry screech. Bright red blood still drips from a rat left on the tree, the hawk's very recent kill.

Nearby, in an area set back from the road next to a small pond, stands a yellow tent with bright red edging. The fabric is thick and of superior quality, providing shelter and comfort from the changeable weather. It is covered with all manner of odds and ends hanging from the awning, and an iron cooking pot bubbles and shakes over a fire. An elderly couple sit comfortably on chairs beside it.

Waving you over, the lady breezily calls out "Come, come, weary traveller. You look hungry!"

They seem genuinely pleased to see another soul on the island, and you are likewise happy for an encounter that is not immediately or apparently dangerous. You approach warily and the man, noticing your hesitation, stands up and holds his hand out to an empty chair by the fire.

"Please, take a seat, we don't get many visitors," he smiles.

If you wish to sit with the couple and rest a while, turn to **116**.

Otherwise, if you want to journey northwest to a crossroads, turn to **59**. If you wish to move southeast to a Y junction, turn to **198**.

168

A single crack accompanies a puff of smoke from the pistol, and the fleeing man collapses in a heap, motionless from your well-aimed shot. A dark red pool spreads on the stone cobbles beneath him, and you hear barely concealed sobbing from among the remaining slaves.

The pirates cheer and clap, and the leader nods, obviously impressed with your aim and, in particular, your ruthlessness.

Add 1 point to the ☉ symbol (A) on your character sheet.

Note you have passed this test and turn to **30**.

169

You stand and brush yourself off. Rotten wooden beams, the cause of the floor's collapse, crumble to dust beneath your feet as you look around the cellar in this brief moment of calm. Soon, the sound of cracking plaster and tiny pieces of stone hitting the floor indicate the upper walls might also be on their way down into the cellar shortly.

To your right, stone stairs lead to the ground floor and away from danger. A heavy, iron-bound wooden door stands opposite the stairs.

If you wish to climb the stairs, turn to **28**. If you wish to open the door, turn to **73**.

170

Although the weather is mild and the conditions fair, the slope offers numerous surprises for an inexperienced climber. The progress is easy on your arms and legs, but the narrow hand and footholds require more delicate efforts to traverse.

Make a check against your Dexterity ability. Add a +2 modifier if you have the Climbing skill.

If you achieve at least 1 success, turn to **125**. If you fail to achieve this, turn to **18**.

171

The beasts hiss and roar as you approach. They look to have taken some punishment since your last visit, as the fresh wounds covering their bodies testify, and one is missing both antennae. They both launch at a surprising speed at you, and you must fight.

	Weapons	Health	
Wounded Giant Beetle	3	1	□
Wounded Giant Beetle	3	2	□

If you wish to escape, add 1 point to the 🔯 symbol (G) on your character sheet. To head west from the clearing, turn to **11**. If you want to escape southeast, turn to **61**.

If you win, turn to **87**.

172

Add the codeword **LUCID**.

You recognise the rock formations on the outcrop match those from the treasure map you found in the abandoned village. You head to the marked spot and straight away see the large peculiar stone inscribed on the map. Moving this solid and heavy rock takes some effort, but you eventually reveal a gap between two larger boulders in which resides a small metal chest, brown from rust, yet well-made and sturdy.

You open the box and inside are several interesting items. Necklaces and rings, a bottle of light greenish blue liquid, plus a heavy sack of coins.

Add **30 Denarii** and **Fine Jewellery [25 Denarii]** to your inventory.

On closer inspection, the bottle has a trident symbol pressed into the wax seal.

Add **Potion of Neptune's Breath [Consumable. Magic]** to your inventory. You may use this item at any point to gain the power of **Water Breathing**.

The power expires at the end of the chapter you gained it, or when you leave this volume.

Having emptied the chest, you must now return northeast to the mainland. Turn to **143**.

173

The thick door to the house is firmly locked, however, the frame is thoroughly rotten and you manage to pull the hinges off without any appreciable effort. You peer into the dusty gloom, but it is dusty and barren. Both rooms in the house are empty of furniture, and you cannot see anything of value other than some empty glass bottles, corks intact.

A flash of movement to your left from the direction of the beamed roof startles you as a spider, its chitinous armoured body wider than your chest, dives straight at your head.

You must fight.

Attacks using the keyword [Water] cause half damage (rounded down).

	Weapons	Health	
Venomous Spidercrab	2	4	

If you are wounded in this combat, the spidercrab's venom remains in your system. Note **Spidercrab Venom (Level 1)** in the Conditions section on your character sheet.

The next time you perform any action, including a rest, that increases your Health by at least 1 point, you can remove the venom from your conditions. You do not gain any Health from this action but further healing then acts as normal.

If you have the Constitution skill, the venom has no effect.

You can use 2 Prayers, and your god's favour removes the effect.

You may escape the combat by exiting the house and moving the door across the entrance. If you wish to do so, add 1 point to the 🛡 symbol (G) on your character sheet and turn to **124**. Do not mark the house as complete.

If you win the fight, turn to **95**.

174

You remove the dagger's oak handle with a solid strike from a heavy rock and jam the metal into a split at the tip of the shaft of wood. The strong grass attaches it securely and you can feel the improvement in both reach and control of your new weapon.

Remove **Dagger [Small Melee +0]**.

Add **Makeshift Spear [Small Melee +1]** to your inventory. If you have the Smithing Skill, you have crafted an improved weapon. Add **Makeshift Spear [Small Melee +2]** to your inventory instead.

Your weapon is now enhanced, you must decide what your next course of action should be.

If you wish to take shelter in the cave, turn to **33**.

To head east inland, turn to **63**.

175

A brutal northern wind, unnatural and violent, batters the island relentlessly. Waves crash against the coast, and the raging waters pummel you hard.

Make a check against your Physical ability.

If you achieve at least 1 success, turn to **108**. If you fail, turn to **38**.

176

Add the codeword **REMIT**.

If you wish to exit west from the clearing, turn to **11**. If you want to travel southeast, turn to **61**.

177

This pathway on the northernmost region of the island runs between the headland and farm through tall, thick brush, reaching chest height in places. The blades move as the sea, undulating as waves in the wind. You proceed forward, arm outstretched to move aside the grassy tendrils.

If you have already marked the box below against the current chapter, turn to **27**.

Otherwise, mark the box below against the current chapter and turn to that section number.

Chapter I, turn to **115**. ☐

Chapter II, turn to **96**. ☐

Chapter III, turn to **5**. ☐

178

The surrounding fields are eerily quiet as you pass, and the wind delivers a low and continuous rustling as it blows across the island and through the dead husks of the crops. Occasionally, you are startled by more pronounced and focused currents of air rattling loose debris across stony ground, but you proceed uninterrupted to your destination.

To continue north to the farm, turn to **141**. To head south to the T junction, turn to **68**.

179

He looks rather disappointed at your refusal but retains his genial smile.

"Sorry, we have not eaten today, please excuse us." he apologises as they both enjoy the stew.

The lady speaks of the hunting opportunities on the island and the dangers that have caused the prey animals to become so especially skittish.

"You need to be very careful else you'll go hungry," she warns.

They finish the contents of the still steaming bowls with speed and the man produces three silver goblets and a tall, thin bottle of red liquid.

"Would you join us in a glass of wine at least?" he offers

If you accept the offer, turn to **97**. If you decline, turn to **40**.

180

Your performance impresses the leader, and he offers his hand to you.

"Good show!" he states in a complimentary and deferential tone. "You should prove a useful member of the crew."

Most of the group shake your hand or firmly slap you on the back, welcoming you to their group.

Add the codeword **KNAVE**.

Their main vessel, anchored off the coast, will leave soon for Neapolis, south of the Imperial Capital. The cost of travel is 40 denarii, but shares of transport profits or loot from captured ships on the journey should mitigate this. They will remain until midway through Chapter III (indicated by an 'A' on the time track). From that point, you must discover another method of escape.

If you stay on the island, your companion, if you have one, will rejoin you when you leave the camp.

To exit this area and head north, turn to **88**. If you wish to proceed west along the coast, turn to **6**.

If you have the money, the time track has not passed midway through Chapter III, and you wish to leave the island now, add 5 ability points and spend them if you wish on improving any secondary abilities. You may save any unused points for later.

Remove **Entry 1 - Escape from Phorbantia** from your journal if it is active.

Remove **40 Denarii** from your inventory.

Add the codeword **INGOT**.

If you have a companion, you smuggle them on the ship that night where they will secure themselves within. They will then travel with you to your next destination.

Increase your Health and Prayers to their maximum values, and remove any effects that expire when you leave a volume. Any companion will now depart your service.

Turn to section **344** in Volume I.

181

Your journey along the wide road is a pleasant yet lengthy walk. The bright sun is high in the sky and its glare catches the brightly coloured foliage, causing you to squint the entire way. This concentrated effort, combined with the substantial trek, leaves you exhausted by the end, but it is nevertheless uneventful.

To travel north, turn to **34**. To go south, turn to **88**.

182

Continuing to chatter for a good length of time, you feel pleasantly warm in the friendly and generous company. Feeling quite stiff in the chair, you half lift yourself up to stretch. Your neck aches and you twist it to smooth the wrinkles in the muscles.

You look up into the sky. It is dark, with a small glimmer of approaching dawn to the east. This is quite unexpected. You are sure you arrived here in the morning, but your memory is not clear at present, and you cannot be certain. The incense is powerful, and your thoughts feel muddled. You close your eyes for a moment and when you open them, it is broad daylight.

You are now feeling quite weary, as if you have travelled a long distance without rest or nourishment. You stand and step back, confused and trying hard to recall where you are. Indeed, you now struggle to remember *who* you are.

An iron cooking pot bubbles and shakes over a fire and an elderly couple sit on stools by it.

Waving you over, the lady calls out "Come, come, weary traveller. You look hungry!"

They seem genuinely pleased to see another soul on the island. You stand confused and the man, noticing your apparent hesitation, stands and holds his hand out to an empty chair by the fire.

"Please, take a seat, we don't get many visitors," he smiles.

Turn to **134**.

183

The last of the critters succumb to your onslaught and all becomes quiet. Muted and distant rustling reminds you that the problem is not wholly solved, but your immediate jeopardy at least has ended.

To progress north to the farm, turn to **141**. To continue south to the T junction, turn to **68**.

184

With your body tired and aching, you finally ascend to the summit of the mountain.

You survey the island. It looks around two miles in length and maybe a mile wide. The forest canopy obscures most of the ground to the south and east, where the more exposed northern area of farmland is clear from your vantage point.

Progressing further onwards, you clamber over some tightly bound branches and dried grass. You now stand in a flat depression with more dead and dried grass.

A silvery glint of metal catches your eye, as does a bright white sphere about 2 feet across with black speckles in the centre of the nest...

Nest! As soon as that realisation dawns on you, an almighty roar screams from above.

You duck as, diving at you from the skies, a giant creature's snapping maw misses you by mere inches.

Staggering at the onslaught, you leap aside as it dives for another attack. The creature is a horrible, winged serpent that hisses and roars as it defends its lair and egg from your encroachment.

You must fight.

	Weapons	Health	
Adult Winged Serpent	4	4	

You cannot escape due to the precarious location of your fight.

If you win, turn to **196**.

185

The path ends at a cove with a rocky sandstone beach. There is nothing of interest here, so you must return east.

Turn to **164**.

186

The skies are dark with the low mist and the air is quiet. The path is undemanding to navigate and a distant screech from what sounds like a hungry gull breaks the peace.

A few moments later, a second call, marginally different to the first and much closer, fills your ears.

You peer into the gloomy skies and hear the deep and rhythmic sound of flapping wings approaching. The tempo increases quicker and quicker as something, or things, prepare to land.

A trio of feathered humanoids dive at you out of the darkness. Their features resemble the Terra Volatis, but are much thinner and with facial features more akin to a hawk than a human.

The speed of their attack knocks you off balance and screeching in angry squawks, they claw and peck at you. You and any companion must fight with a modifier of -2 to your Weapons and Mystical abilities for the first two rounds of combat.

	Weapons	Health	
Aer Volas	2	1	☐
Aer Volas	1	1	☐
Aer Volas	2	1	☐

You may not escape as the creatures are too nimble and fast to evade.

If you win, turn to **145**.

187

The dark rocks at the water's edge are black following the rain, and the thick bushes and shrubs in the area have grown fat with the downpour. They pulsate in the wind and driving storm.

You climb a large protruding boulder as you carefully negotiate the path, and grab hold of a bush that sways on top.

A sharp pain courses through your hand as the plant wraps its tentacle-like branches around your wrist, and you yank it away. The bush has you held tight, but you rip your arm away again with success this time, leaving small chunks of skin and flesh attached to the thorns.

To both your left and right, more plants approach, the thorned branches pointing at you like outstretched arms, eager to enter a deadly embrace.

You must fight these carnivorous shrubs.

	Weapons	Health	
Carnivorous Shrub	1	3	☐
Carnivorous Shrub	1	3	☐
Carnivorous Shrub	1	4	☐

The lumbering plants move at a crawling pace, and you can escape if needed. If you wish to retreat, add 1 point to the 🛡 symbol (G) on your character sheet. To move north from this location, turn to **100**. To proceed south, turn to **143**.

If you win, turn to **157**.

188

You are at a T junction.

The path winds eastwards around the north face of the island's highest peak. To the south, it continues a short way before splitting again at another junction. To the west, the trail drops towards the sea.

If you want to go east, turn to **7**. To head south, turn to **85**. To travel west, turn to **135**.

189

Add the codeword **URBAN**.

You pull the rowboat up to the rocks and secure the lines. It appears a substantial battle must have raged in this area not too long ago as cargo, pieces of shattered hull, and broken masts litter the shore. A quick search reveals nothing of value among the wreckage.

There is one path leading east up a steep incline deeper into the island, and you begin your climb. Turn to **164**.

190

You are at a T junction. To the northwest, the path winds up a hill into a dark, densely forested area. Southeast, the trail narrows and drops towards a small bay. To the southwest, it skirts around the southern edge of a light golden-brown leafed wood.

If you wish to head northwest, turn to **61**. To go southeast, turn to **151**. If you want to move southwest, turn to **110**.

191

Your journey along the coast is uneventful. The cool breeze of the sea tempers the heat of the beating sun's rays, making the lengthy trek quite pleasant.

To proceed east, turn to **17**. To continue west, turn to **143**.

192

Add the codeword **MINOR**.

The skeleton collapses and you step over to investigate the pile of bones.

It has a worn leather pouch strapped across its back, along with a bow. You open the pouch and find a purse containing some red crystals, a few sticks of charcoal, and a map of an island called 'Phorbantia' with some cryptic notes and strange symbols. There is a quiver of arrows nearby.

Add **10 Red Crystals [Fire]** and **Shortbow [Large Ranged +1]** to your inventory.

Turn to **200**.

193

You examine the skies which, dark and brooding as they are, show no signs of storms. Still, the tingling on your skin gets stronger.

Without warning, a single bolt of blue lightning erupts from the ground and passes close enough to burn you.

Roll one die and lose that amount of Health. This is the equivalent of a single combat attack, and the damage is reduced by armour, agility, or other items and powers as it would be in combat.

You force yourself to leap forward, charging out of the clearing as several other bolts blast upwards at the forest canopy.

Make a check against your Agility ability to avoid further injury. If you fail to gain at least 1 success, take a further attack with 1 die of Health loss from a second blast.

To journey west, turn to **34**. To progress east, turn to **82**.

194

You carefully aim the pistol at the captain's head and pull the trigger. His face explodes in a red mist as the lead shot passes through his skull, leaving small chunks of brain on the horrified and blood-covered face of the nearest pirate.

Falling heavily to the ground, the body twitches once and lies motionless on the floor.

The pirates turn to you in shock, and you lunge forward, taking them utterly by surprise. In the distance, the slave escapes in the commotion.

Add 1 point to the 🔻 symbol (W) on your character sheet. When you turn to the next section, note that the Pirate Captain is already dead and counts towards the total of 6 required to be killed in that combat.

Turn to **65**.

195

You stroll with confidence to the nearest pirate, a young human female with a wicked scar running across her throat. Standing in front of her, you smile as you put your hands calmly on your hips.

Your poised approach visibly confuses the surprised woman who calls to a broad young man with long blonde hair, and sporting a bright red tunic. "Look who we got here." she exclaims, pointing to you.

The man strides over to you and sizes your profile. He seems impressed by your build and your self-assured advance.

"Hail stranger. We could do with someone who's not afraid to walk into danger."

He pauses, musing his options for a second, and you are keenly aware of the other pirates surrounding you in a circle.

"What say we give you a couple of little tests? Nothing too taxing, and if you pass, you can buy into our little enterprise here. If you fail, well...."

He nods over his shoulder at the line of slaves, bound and naked, shivering with fear in the dirt.

Turn to **123**.

196

The serpent lets out one final screech of rage as it dies.

The battle now won, you approach the shining metal and find it is the binding of a sturdy shield still attached to the arm of a human skeleton.

You also discover a small leather pouch containing some coins hidden among a pile from another of the beast's unfortunate meals, an interesting humanoid creature with a beaked face and wings.

Add **5 Denarii** and **Medium Wooden Shield [Shield. Light Armour +2]** to your inventory.

Add the codeword **HALVE**.

There is nothing further of value in the nest and you descend the mountain. To go east, turn to **90**, to journey west, turn to **46**.

197

The open road offers little in the way of protection against the driving rain. However, it is a solidly built thoroughfare of cobblestones and quality mortar, and despite its age, it gives you no difficulty on your journey.

To continue north, turn to **34**. To head south, turn to **88**.

198

You arrive at a Y junction.

To the north, the path heads into a dark and dense wood, and you are sure you can hear distant screaming from within. Northwest, the path passes between two forested areas towards the eastern part of a high mountainous area. To the south, you can see several ruined buildings.

If you wish to travel north into the dark wood, turn to **24**. To proceed northwest, turn to **167**. If you want to move south towards the ruins, turn to **34**.

199

The clearing where you fought the giant beetles is quiet and you pass through with no incident. The bodies are gone, dragged into the undergrowth and consumed by scavengers no doubt.

If he is not your companion, Regulus, the peregrine alta you first encountered here, kneels in prayer. You can add him as a companion for no cost. Go to the Companions section at the end of the book and note his abilities, equipment, and skills on your character sheet.

Add the codeword GRADE if Regulus joins you.

He will accompany you for no cost while you remain in this volume. He will depart from your service should you leave the volume.

Any companion travelling with you will head back to their usual location.

If you wish to exit the clearing and go west, turn to **11**. If you wish to head southeast, turn to **61**.

The map is highly detailed and carefully produced by someone with a keen talent and obvious knowledge of the area. If you want to refer to the map you have found in future, make a note of the section number you are reading and return to this page.

You are unsure what the strange symbols mean, but the Roman numerals are familiar to anyone born in these lands. A handy reference guide is on the next page, in Appendix A, translating all values between 1 and 100 into Roman numerals. In this table, you will see the very first entry on the map, LXXXIX, is the number 89.

It puzzles you that the short amount of ground you have covered does not suggest this island receives much in the way of rain. The dry, rocky ground would make it difficult for trees to grow, yet lush and vibrant forests flourish in the distance.

The map also shows forested areas inland and you guess its proximity to the events on Sicilia are most likely the cause.

To continue west towards the sea, turn to **118**. To travel east to a T junction, turn to **68**.

Appendix A
Roman Numerals 1-100

1	I	26	XXVI	51	LI	76	LXXVI
2	II	27	XXVII	52	LII	77	LXXVII
3	III	28	XXVIII	53	LIII	78	LXXVIII
4	IV	29	XXIX	54	LIV	79	LXXIX
5	V	30	XXX	55	LV	80	LXXX
6	VI	31	XXXI	56	LVI	81	LXXXI
7	VII	32	XXXII	57	LVII	82	LXXXII
8	VIII	33	XXXIII	58	LVIII	83	LXXXIII
9	IX	34	XXXIV	59	LIX	84	LXXXIV
10	X	35	XXXV	60	LX	85	LXXXV
11	XI	36	XXXVI	61	LXI	86	LXXXVI
12	XII	37	XXXVII	62	LXII	87	LXXXVII
13	XIII	38	XXXVIII	63	LXIII	88	LXXXVIII
14	XIV	39	XXXIX	64	LXIV	89	LXXXIX
15	XV	40	XL	65	LXV	90	XC
16	XVI	41	XLI	66	LXVI	91	XCI
17	XVII	42	XLII	67	LXVII	92	XCII
18	XVIII	43	XLIII	68	LXVIII	93	XCIII
19	XIX	44	XLIV	69	LXIX	94	XCIV
20	XX	45	XLV	70	LXX	95	XCV
21	XXI	46	XLVI	71	LXXI	96	XCVI
22	XXII	47	XLVII	72	LXXII	97	XCVII
23	XXIII	48	XLVIII	73	LXXIII	98	XCVIII
24	XXIV	49	XLIX	74	LXXIV	99	XCIX
25	XXV	50	L	75	LXXV	100	C

Appendix B
Vol 0 Companion

Name: Regulus

Race: Peregrine Alta

God: None

Abilities

Mystical   2

Weapons   2

Knowledge   2

Social   1

Max Health   10

Skills: Melee Weapons

Inventory

8 Clear [Air] Crystals

Spear [Small Melee +2]

Scalemail [Light Armour +3]

Background

Regulus is an intelligent and reliable ally who has spent many decades in the Empire's service, and is expertly informed in its politics and machinations. He rarely speaks, preferring to keep opinions to himself unless directly asked, yet any words he does offer are well thought out and efficiently delivered.

He will not leave the island and will depart your service should you find your way off Phorbantia.

Behaviour. Will use crystals for combat spells if instructed. Will only use crystals for healing himself when he reaches Health of 3 or below. He will only use crystals to heal the character in combat should they reach Health of 3 or below, and the character has no other healing available.

Notes

If Regulus dies, turn to section **70** in Volume 0.

Rules Summary

Symbols

Full rest location	Short rest location	Journal entry	Expansion link

Resting

Full Rest - Add 2 markers to the time track. Restore all health and prayers to the character and companion. Gain **Well Rested [Any Ability +1]** power. Spend ability points on improving secondary abilities.

Short Rest - Add 1 marker to the time track. Raise the character's Health to 10 (14 with Survival skill). Increase companion's Health by half their Max Health, rounded down. All regain 1 Prayer per level of Lore.

Ability Checks

Roll dice equal to the modified value of that ability. Score one success for each roll of 4+.

If the modified ability is 0, roll one die and score one success on a roll of 5+.

Bonuses from items, spells, or powers do not stack. Use the highest value unless there is a negative modifier, status buff, or other modifier in the section containing the ability check. There are applied separately.

Combat

Order of action.

1) Character and any companions or allies each take one action in any order. Additional actions are also taken in any order.

2) Enemies each take one action in the order they are shown in the text.

A combatant may use one action:

- Perform an attack on one opponent.
- Swap one weapon.
- Use an item.
- Use one consumable or power.
- Use a unique mastery.
- Cast a combat spell.
- Escape.

Attack. Number of dice rolled = Weapons ability.

One success on each roll of 4+ with weapon proficiency. 5+ without weapon proficiency, unarmed, or at level 0 in the Weapons ability.

Additional defensive bonus with unmodified Agility ability of 3 or higher, Number of dice rolled = Half of the modified Agility ability, rounded down.

Reduce number of successes by 1 on the roll of:

      6+ Light Armour and/or Shield

      5+ No Armour

      No successes removed for Heavy Armour

Armour rating defensive bonus. Number of dice rolled = Armour Rating. Reduce number of successes by 1